STORIES TO S[HARE WITH]
MY PAR[TNER]
BOOK 2

MW00342126

A BOOK OF STORIES TO ENJOY TOGETHER!

ISBN: 978-0-6452639-5-4 (Paperback Print)

ISBN: 978-0-6452639-7-8 (Kindle)

ISBN: 978-0-6452639-6-1 (Paperback Large Print)

ISBN: 978-0-6452639-8-5 (E-pub)

ISBN: 978-0-6452639-9-2 (Audiobook)

ABOUT THIS BOOK

This book is an anthology of made-up short stories and may contain a few poems. Most of these stories are an accumulation of yarns I wrote while taking part in a writers' group in Camden, New South Wales, either in our spontaneous writing sessions or as 'homework'.

There is no rhyme or logical reason to the stories or their purpose other than to, hopefully, make you smile and enjoy them while doing your thing on the toilet.

They are short with each story taking less than four-minutes to read, so in and out I say and off to do other things.

ACKNOWLEDGEMENTS

Foremost, I wish to acknowledge the spiritual and moral support I received from my wife.

I dedicate this book to you, Red!

Without this support, and the many breakfasts, lunches, and dinners she has cooked for me in our twenty-odd years of marriage together, I would not have the strength to sit in front of a screen and pound the keys.

Second, a big thank you to the writing group members, my companions in the writing trenches who have given me instruction and courage to put pen to paper and help me through the years.

TABLE OF CONTENTS

MY FIRST BOOK..1

MY FIRST SUIT 5

MY BIGGEST SECRET.. 8

MY TOWN LIBRARY... 9

NEITHER WILL YOU 11

PASSING THE BUCK 12

RETIREMENT PLAN 14

SALAD DAYS..17

SCIENCE FICTION WRITERS OF THE FUTURE.......18

SECOND VERSE SAME AS THE FIRST.......................20

SISTER KATE 22

THE DEFENDERS..24

THE HAMMER OF THOR..26

THE OBLIVIOUS WRITER..27

THE OUTWORLDERS...29

THE PASSAGE OF VENUS..31

THE POWER OF INSIGHT..34

THE RIGHT LIFE PARTNER IN TINDER 35

THE SHORTEST DAY 37

THE HAPPY VALLEY AGENCY FOR TIME TRAVEL...39

TOOTHPICKS 43

GENUINE FRIENDSHIP 44

WEREWOLVES OF HAPPY VALLEY.............................49

WHAT IF HE SAID YES...52

WHAT WAS WRITTEN ON THE SIGN INTO THE BEAR PARK?
....53

WHO DOES ANYWAY? 55

CAN YOU NOTICE? 58

BRING IT ON! 59

IT SEEMED LIKE A CLEVER IDEA AT THE TIME 62

IT WAS A SHOCKING NOISE 65

MARCH FORTH! 67

MEMORIES 68

NEXT TIME, CHEW MORE 69

SCAMS 71

THE AZRAEL KEY 73

THE BETRAYAL..75

THE CHAIR MAN 76

THE GREAT BATTLE 81

THE GREAT ESCAPE 84

THE MOST UNUSUAL JOB I EVER HAD 87

THE PHOTOGRAPH 90

THE TRAIN JOURNEY 93

THE WHITE BEARDED ONE 94

THERE IS ALWAYS NEXT YEAR 95

WAS THAT REALLY THE EASTER BUNNY? 96

YOU CAN'T NAME YOUR BABY THAT! 98

YOUR OWN CHOICE 100

A BRIEF ENCOUNTER..101

A GRAND ADVENTURE AWAITS...102

A SENSE OF GUILT 104

BIRTHDAY PRESENT 105

JOIN THE TEAM..107

I SEE NOTHING BUT RED 108

IN THE COFFEE SHOP 110

LISTEN TO YOUR HEART 112

PARALYSED WITH FEAR 113

ST. PATRICKS' DAY 114

THE BLUE WOOLLEN COAT 116

THE COLLECTOR 118

TWO OF ME 121

WHY DO I ENJOY WRITING 122

ABOUT THE AUTHOR 123

MY FIRST BOOK

For the past year and a half, I have been taking part in the Northport Author Group, which meets in the local Northport Library once a month for an entire day of discussions and writing skills symposiums. This morning was no different. Our meeting starts at 10 AM and runs through 4 PM with a lunch hour break. While I was waiting in the library reading area for our room to open, I heard: 'Psst. I can get you everything cheap' I turn and find standing close behind me a bespectacled man smiling like a Cheshire cat.

'What do you mean?' I answered, worried but intrigued. I had been working on my main character (a burglar) series of stories for over a year hoping to see if I can make the stories into a novel of some type, or at least an anthology, and I use the solitude of the library to accomplish this when the man interrupts my thoughts. Aggravated by the intruder and yet intrigued. I pressed the conversation.

'Again, what do you mean by you can get everything for me cheap?'

The man pulls up a chair and in a low voice says, 'I mean everything you need to get an ISBN. I got it. You need an ISSN number; I also have it; you need to have books printed, it's in the bag.', the smiling, bespectacled man said.

'What in the world is an ISSN number or even an ISBN? What do I need them for?' I ask.

'Well, my friend, whether you need one, or the other, depends on what you plan to do with your novel there.' pointing to my pile of handwritten papers.

'Explain to me the difference,' I said.

'An ISBN or International Standard Book Number is a numeric, thirteen-digits, commercial book identifier which is unique for each of the books you write. You are going to write over one book, right?' questioned the man. 'Yes,' I answered, but as immersed in intrigue as ever.

'The ISSN is an International Standard Serial Number, an eight-digit serial number used to identify a serial publication.', responded the man.

'So, do you intend to publish a book, not a serial? Which is it?' he asks again. 'Well, maybe a book, yes. Not sure yet. In that case,' the man says, 'get both, and you are in better shape to do what you want to do when you decide. What do you think?', he pressed me for an answer.

'Gosh, I am confident I will write more novels, at least I think I am and publish them, even if I do the publishing myself, so I guess I need the ISBN. How much?' I pressed my question.

'A small cost of $45.00 for you, my friend, for the first unique number, then if you want more, again just $45.00 each. What you think? Have we got a deal?'

My thoughts were flying through my mind; '$45.00 seemed reasonable for the first and then $45.00 again. What can I lose? Yes, you got yourself a deal.' I smiled and shook his hand.

The bespectacled man then asks; 'Now how about the printing of your book, any ideas on how you are going to do it and the quantity you might want?'

No, I had not thought about it honestly as a matter of fact I had thought very little about it, but then I thought with family, friends and maybe even hooking up with a small independent bookstore in the Northport area, I might sell at least one hundred books, so I say; 'I need one hundred books. How much?'

The smiling man said, 'Wait one minute. It takes a lot of questions to decide on the printing of a book.'

'Let's start with the size. Any idea there?' the man asks me.

My answer was, 'None, what do you recommend?'

'Well, I find a handy size is an A5 size which is 210mm x 148mm with a white and black paper in paperback format with a perfect bound glued spine with a colour laminated cover and around 150 pages. Would this be OK for your first publication?'

I gave it some thought.

Again, I had not realised that so much detail was necessary to publish a book. When you see books in libraries and bookstores, they are there; you never wonder the process a book goes through to become a physical book. You may think of the effort that the writer, the proofreader, the editor, illustrator, and many others go through, but not the physical creation of the book itself, never, so I learned something today.

'Yes, that would be great. How much to have the books produced and delivered to me in Northport?'

'For you, my friend, the cost is $45.00 for one ISBN and the printing, delivery and GST another $1,445.00. All you have to do is think of a selling price per book, and you are a published writer!' The satisfied bespectacled man answers.

This action will deplete my bank account by $1,490.00, but if I could get, say, $25 per book, which would be a gross $2,500.00 minus the $1,490.00, netting me my first profit of $1,010.00. Not too shabby, I thought.

The man, again repeating himself and smiling, says; 'For one hundred books printed and delivered to your home, the cost is $1,490.00, including your IBSN number. What do you think, deal?'

Again, we shook hands on the deal, and the man agreed to send me an invoice for the books to which he states I can pay upon delivery and inspection. As he walked out of the library, I thought to myself; 'Way too easy?' I never attended that day's meeting of the Northport Author Group. I was too excited.

In a week, I see a delivery van pull up in front of my home and the delivery driver unloads four boxes. Before the delivery man can ring the doorbell, I open the door and welcome the delivery of my 'babies.' Sign for the delivery, and I carry each box into my dining area, where I place the first box on the table and the rest on the floor. I cut the top of the box, making sure I do not injure my babies inside.

The cover is just magnificent. I got a free photo of an old Northport (in glorious back and white), showing an old farm and made it part of my cover. The title of the book, 'Northport Stories; Old and New' inscribed along the bottom in bold red, fixating anyone's eyes to it. I was in love already and perish the thought of having to give away or even sell them, for as I mentioned, they are my 'babies.'

'No,' I said to myself; 'These are fruits for my money-making dream and future glory as a writer. I will part from them and hope to write more.' I sat at my computer, enter the details to pay the invoice and push the Pay key. 'I am ready for business,' I said to myself.

The next morning, I ventured into the Northport Central Business District and targeted the three local bookstores to see if the owner/manager would care to take the books on consignment. The first bookstore was a total failure. It is part of one of those mega-chains that had umpteen vice-presidents in charge of everything, and for a person to get an appointment for a meeting, hell has to freeze over.

My second bookstore proved a little more welcome but also not a success. It was a used bookstore, and the manager said he could take maybe five books and buy them from me for two dollars each. 'The books are not used. They are new.' I declined the offer and walked toward my last hope.

'Missy's Book Shop,' in the Paragon Arcade was this adorable little bookstore owned by Ms. Missy Kottar. Ms. Kottar had to be in her early seventies but dressed as a ray of sunshine and, when we spoke, a spark is felt in the air when she expresses herself. I introduced myself to Ms. Missy and told her of my dream of becoming a published writer. OK, I was self-published one at that. I recounted my start in writing, and my future dreams as Ms. Missy stood there behind her little counter and listened, smiled, and nodded her head.

When I finished my discourse, she said; 'Sonny, that was one hell of a yarn, and mean truly enjoyed it. So much that I will give you a chance in my humble little store for you to sell your books, I will give you some space over in the historical section, and another little of space in the fiction section for let's say, ten books each, what do you say?'

I did not know what to say. I got no one to help me in my endeavour. So, what could I say, 'Yes, fantastic! When do I bring in the books?'

'Wait a minute sonny, let's discuss finances.' Oh, oh, here it comes. I can see my profits just disappearing, I thought.

Ms. Missy said: 'I have been in this business for 40 years and have a pretty good idea of what prices should be for a self-publishing author, so I want to be fair.' I listen. 'I have plenty of expense running this shop, and as you can see by my opening hours, they cover only four hours per day Monday to Saturday, for I go to church on Sunday and rest the Lord's Day. So, I have a two-prong proposition for you. I will pay you $18 per book, sell it for $30, and I believe that should you cover your costs, and we both make a little profit. How does that sound, for starters?'

I thought was that it was a fair deal Ms. Missy was offering me, so I agree. Then Ms. Missy said, 'My other proposition is that you come in and run the shop for me an additional four hours a day, Monday to Saturday, thus making sure I am open eight hours a day and we both rest on Sunday. Is this deal palatable to you?'

I stood there and thought this through. I thought it would engross my life as an author in my paperwork, sitting in solitude in the library and considering ideas for stories. I did not envision working twenty-four hours a week in a bookstore where my books would be on display and available for sale. There were some cons to the proposition. My writing time diminish, but there were some pros also in the proposal. I could see folks come into the store, see their browsing behaviours and purchasing habits, meet interesting individuals and maybe explore some ideas for more stories. My answer was: 'You got yourself a deal, Ms. Missy.'

It has been now twenty-seven years since my meeting with Ms. Missy, who has since passed. I own 'Missy's Book Shop,' and as I stand behind my little counter, just like Ms. Missy did when I first saw her, I wonder when some young novelist will walk in to speak to me about their first book.

MY FIRST SUIT

'But I do not want to go to Miss Arancini to get my first suit, Mother. I want to go to Whitman's.' I implored my mother. You see next week I was going to start my first job in Happy Valley at the Commercial Banking Company of Sydney or the C. B. C. Bank as it was more commonly known as a teller officer trainee at its branch in Happy Valley New South Wales (NSW).

I was excited having just completed my schooling at the Happy Valley Public School. I was ready to start my apprenticeship at the C.B.C. Bank and I wanted to look as sharp as ever, hence my insistence of a new suit at Whatman's'. Mother had other ideas. 'No Walter, you will go today and get measured by Miss Arancini for your new suit, and that is it, young man. Do I need to speak to your father about this?'

That was the end of the conversation, and so I settled because Miss Arancini was going to tailor my first suit.

Is not that I did not like Miss Arancini, well I did not dislike her, but then she was a strange sort of woman. An ancient woman of forty-eight years of age, well, that is what the townsfolk said. She never married and lived in a particular looking building since the day she was born. Seldom did you see her in the shops and at church. Rumours were that folks saw strange lights going on and off at her place at night and when neighbours complained to Constable Brightman, he would knock on Miss Arancini's door, ask what was happening and walk back to the station and report; 'All is well at Miss Arancini.' None ever bother even trying to find out her surname. Everyone knew her as Miss Arancini. Maybe she did not have a surname, I thought. Anyway, people gave up complaining. She did not do any harm, so what if she was strange?

When we arrive at Miss Arancini's house, she welcomed us with some fresh scones and tea. Miss Arancini said: 'It is always nice to meet one's client before getting down to business.' A strange saying, but her scones are delicious, and a nice cup of tea settles anyone's nerves.

'So, what do you want, young man?' Asks Miss Arancini. Before I even open my mouth, Mother interjects: 'He needs a modest looking grey suit. Nothing fancy. Something we can afford to go with his new white shirt and his father's old tie. I do not want to spend a lot of money.' I guess my needs and wants will not be listened to today, so I just smiled at Miss Arancini, and she smiled back.

'Leave it with me, Mrs. Campbell. I know what the young man needs. If you can come back in a couple of hours, I will finish with all my measurements, and he can then return home with you for dinner.' Said Miss Arancini.

'Splendid, I shall return at 5 M to pick up Walter then.' Said Mother placing a peck on the cheek, how embarrassing, and exits the house.

'Now Walter, tell me what YOU want in a suit.' Miss Arancini whispers to me.

I was taken by surprise since no one ever asked me for my opinion, I stood there with my mouth open for a minute until these words came out: 'I want to look, feel and be successful in the suit you are tailoring for me, Miss Arancini! May I ask you a question, Miss Arancini?'

'But of course, young Walter, what is it?'

'Your name Arancini, it is kind of funny name for a girl. How did you get it?' Walters asks.

'Well Walter, my great grandmother's maternal grandmother's name was Arachne, and she was a skilled weaver many, many years ago. All the women in my family take our first name from her or a variation of it. Now. It is my turn. How old are you, Walter, if I may ask?' Miss Arancini spoke to me.

'I am fifteen years of age and finished my schooling with honours in mathematics, thus receiving a well-deserved appointment as a teller officer trainee at the C. B. C. Bank,' I exclaimed.

'How about if I tailor for you an exceptional suit that will make you so successful from your first day that by the time you reach your twenty-four birthday you will be the president of the C. B. C. Bank. You would like that?' Miss Arancini states.

'You make it sound like you are making me a magic suit, Miss Arancini,' I said, chuckling a bit. 'I will do just that, young Walter. So, let's get started.' For the next hour, Miss Arancini measures me as well as possible. Taking measurements from the neck, chest, shoulder width, arm length, bicep circumference, wrists circumference, stomach circumference, back length, waistline, hip circumference, inside leg, thigh and then Miss Arancini asked me to choose the fit I would like the most: comfort, regular, slim, I was not sure, so I choose comfort to which she said: 'Excellent choice, smart young man.'

Miss Arancini finishes taking all the measurements and asks me to sit next to her on her divan, which I did. She takes a small breath and says to me: 'Walter, the suit I will tailor for you will be of the best material in the world, but what makes it special is how I handle the thread as I weave the cloth to make this suit. It will be special since the material is a modest grey, as your mother dictated, but the colour of the suit will change each week from the first day you put it on. Not only will it change colour, but it will grow as you grow, so it will always fit you. This suit will make you look, feel and be successful in your banking career. All you have to do is to be imaginative with the answers that people will ask you about the suit because they will think you have many suits. Do you understand me?'

I just nodded to Miss Arancini as she continues.

'The suit will also change in style because young Walter style changes year on years. Some years, there will be smaller lapels, larger belt lines, etc, but you will always be in fashion and successful. This is what you want, right, Walter?' she asks.

'Yes, of course. It is what I want; thank you very much Miss Arancini.' I respond.

'Good, this will remain our secret forever.' She said and got up just as the doorbell rang at 5 PM, the anointed time for us to return home.

It has now been nine years since that day. I sometimes walk by Miss Arancini's house to see if I can get a glimpse of her on the way to a visit to one of the many branches that I have responsibility for. To this day, I have not figured out how she knew I would become president of the C.B.C. Bank.

Perhaps I never will.

MY BIGGEST SECRET

The last person who made me smile was on the 10 o'clock news bulletin last night, sharing with the entire community one of my biggest scares.

There on the small screen, well it was an 85-inch screen so not so small, was Sarah, my sister, being interviewed by the local TV newsreader and she was explaining how we became lost.

Lost, we were for sure.

We found ourselves on some dirt road in the middle of nowhere, devoid of all life, it seemed. The GPS was not working, the mobile phone had no little bars at all, and the old 1988 UBD City Directory was not to be trusted. Well, at least not in 2019.

We saw a single level extensive building next to a large house, which gave us hope we would be at least in contact with some civilisation. Then we came upon the rear of the buildings, and while the single level large extensive building was in darkness, there was one room lit in the house, its light emitting from a lower rear window.

We stopped the car and walked up to the house, which stood silent in the night, just the little light shining through the lower window. A beacon of hope, I thought. As we inched our way toward the house, Sarah decides she will be the one that peeks through the window since she is taller than me.

She turns, grabs my arm and yells; 'Run!'.

Let me state here that I seldom listen to my older sister, but this time my feet responded quicker than my head, and I was running faster than Sarah, leaving her behind. We ran and ran. Sarah scared out of her mind while I was just running as I was told to do. We get into the car and once it started, we blast our way onto an asphalt road that was in the building's front and house. As I turn left onto the road, I notice a small flashing sign, 'Bates Motel.'

Sarah is explaining all this to the local TV newsreader, ensuring that she described specific points to the TV viewing audience. Aspects such as she is taller than me; that I ran faster than her; that I seemed a bit more scare that she was, (not true). All these themes very pointed out to the viewing audience, ensuring that all my friends knew of my 'heroics' that night.

As I sit in my lounge watching the news and Sarah belittles me in front of our entire community, I smile, knowing that she soiled her knickers that night as she peeked into that window of the house next to the Bates Motel.

I will never tell on my older sister. That will be my biggest secret.

MY TOWN LIBRARY

The clouds turn grey, and the sky changes into a strange colour of green. The air is pungent, as if rain is coming and then the tornado strikes without warning.

My town is in shambles. All buildings on Main Street are in a mess. Nothing could hold back the fierce spinning wind that took my town away and yet…

There it stands, the library unscathed, not even a broken window.

The library is a surreal magnet in a sea of devastation. The beige building stands with its doors closed as if nothing has happened. I can see that the library has lights on inside, all lit up as if nothing had occurred. I can see people inside. All dressed in different outfits as if from different eras and agitated as if trying to communicate with each other.

Checking the front door, I find it unlocked, so I venture in, and to my astonishment there in front of me I see Napoleon, with twelve of his 'Grande Armee', all confused, speaking out loud to what has to be a unicorn. I see Abraham Lincoln, speaking with Winston Churchill. To their left, I find Bugs Bunny chewing on a carrot while carrying on a conversation with Jessica Rabbit. A nameless cowboy stands close by, twirling his lasso.

The tornado must have caused the book characters to come to life and confined them to the library. My first thought is that I could not unleash these unfortunate characters into the modern world. They would be misunderstood and taken to laboratories for experimentation to find out if there was such a thing as another dimension. I must do something.

If a tornado caused this event, then a second tornado might rectify it. I ran to the children's section and found all the book- cases empty and all the books scattered over the place.

The one pattern I had observed was that if a book had been thrown off the shelf and landed open, the main character of said book had come to life, but if the book fell on the floor unopened, then no character from the book had appeared. I was so glad that 'Jurassic Park' by Michael Crichton landed closed.

Also closed is 'The Wizard of Oz' by L. Frank Baum. I find the page where the tornado takes Dorothy and Toto, and I throw it to the floor. A second tornado springs from the pages, and I run out of the library, past all the surprised book characters, and close the door behind me.

I hear a tremendous roar coming from inside the library and screaming, but in a matter of seconds, all becomes quiet. Some townsfolk

9

gather in front of the library as I go to the front door, open it and the library is all organised, clean, and ready for its patrons to enjoy the wonders of reading again.

NEITHER WILL YOU

Roses are red and violets are blue.

This is my first attempt at a poem for you.

It might not be pretty.

It might not be witty

It might not make any sense.

It may not stand the passage of time.

But remember, darling.

Neither will you.

PASSING THE BUCK

'You want me to do what?' I yelled at Sargent Max Trevor IV.

'I need to take care of the last two Buck-Day Cicadas. They are the last two in existence, and they need to be protected.'

'Sargent, these are just bugs, right? Why do we need to protect them? If, as you said, they are the last two, why bother?'

'Soldier, your job is to follow orders, not to question me. It is imperative that make sure these two last Buck-Day Cicadas survive and repopulate this part of Texas.'

'Sir, yes Sir,' answers the soldier. 'I have one little question, Sir?'

'What is, soldier?' replied the Sargent.

'If we are to make sure they repopulate this part of Texas, how do we know they will, Sir?'

'What do you mean, soldier?'

'Well Sir, these two have they been checked?'

The Sargent looks at the soldier and asks; 'What do you mean, soldier?'

'Well Sir, has anyone checked to see if we have here two boy cicadas, or two girl Cicadas or one boy Cicada and one girl Cicada?'

'That is a damn good question, soldier. I believe you will go places in this man's army. Why don't you check and see what they are?'

'Yes, Sir, and how do I do that?' The perplexed soldier asks.

'Well, boy, turn them upside down and see if there is something underneath that tells you which is which. It should be simple enough.'

'Sargent sir, are we not getting a little personal here?'

'Soldier, you are a member of the United States of America army, the biggest, the best dang army in the world. You should be able to do this task without question. Ask no more questions, follow orders and do it!' screams the Sargent at the poor soldier.

The soldier does as he is told, turns the cicadas upside down and looks in the bottom of the cicadas, and immediately, they both start singing.

'Sargent, sir, we have two male Buck-Day Cicadas here. They cannot repopulate this part of Texas.' proclaims the soldier.

The Sargent takes a few minutes to consider his predicament and how to solve this situation and comes up with the solution.

'Soldier, take the two Buck-Day Cicadas, place them in a box with air holes and ship them to the United States Air Force. They will handle the issue now.'

'Yes sir, but how does this resolve the situation?' asks the soldier.

'It does not resolve it, soldier. I called it passing the buck.' answer the Sargent.

RETIREMENT PLAN

The morning started as most mornings begin at my house, in complete darkness. The first rays of sunlight will not creep through the blinds for another forty minutes, or so and yet I am awake, and then I realise I did not have to go to work today or for that manner, tomorrow either. I am now redundant from my job, and now I lie in bed wondering what my day will be like today.

They do not appreciate us. We go to work every day, Monday through Friday, to do the same routine every day. I am sure the reader can relate.

Who has not awoken every morning gone through the morning rituals, had a shower, eaten breakfast, gone down to the bus stop, and waited for the infernal thing to arrive. You pay for your morning ride using your electronic card, get off at the usual stop and walk the last twenty minutes to the behemoth building that houses your office space at the Allied United Insurance Company in the Happy Valley Central Business District.

I did all that for thirty-seven years, each day as I went over applicants' forms applying for life insurance policies on themselves, their spouses, children and one, for the life of me I could not to this day wonder why an applicant would want their life insurance policy funds go to his dog once he passed away, but if approved, that is exactly what the Allied Insurance Company would do. One mighty lucky dog for sure, I thought.

As a senior underwriter, I verified all aspects of the application form. All data were checked and double-checked. From the information, I would verify the name, birthday, sex of the applicant to all the nitty-gritty for their health, both mental and physical. I approved the underwriting of the policy for the company and thus made the Allied United Insurance Company liable for the claims when they came into the company.

Today, however, was different. I was not working.

Yesterday at 4:45 PM, I arrived at the office of Mr Wilfred Nichols, first vice president of underwriting to be told that my services are no longer in need by the Allied United Insurance Company. Mr Wilfred Nichols tells me I should return to my desk, pick up any personal items and return all ID's to the security guard standing next to Mr Nichols, who would then escort me out of the building.

'What reason am I being let go for?' I asked.

'The underwriting process is going to be now performed using artificial intelligence (AI), which will expedite the process even more efficiently than any human can do.' Responded Mr Nichols.

'So underwriting is now going to be done by machines?' I quipped.

'Not only underwriting but claims as well. We will expedite all our applications and claims and increasing our turnaround time, thus improving our services at a lower cost, which will mean more profits for the company. From application to the processing of the claims, the AI system will verify all forms once the system receives them. Then the claims are verified for completion, and processed and the claim, if applicable, is processed, declined, or paid, without a hitch.'

'And will you pass these savings on the customer's policies?' I asked.

'That is not a concern of yours now. Please go with the security guard and collect your things.' answered Mr Nichols.

So here I am, a fifty-seven-year-old male who missed his pension age requirement by three years because of this premature redundancy and with no other experience in the business world other than underwriting life insurance policies.

It might surprise the reader that I am not worried at all under these circumstances. Twenty-four years ago, with introduction computers there was a massive redundancy program at the Allied United Insurance Company which reduce the number of underwriters from over two hundred to the forty-three that are employed now, of course minus one, me. I do not know if the company would keep any of the remaining forty-two, but that is not my problem.

Twenty-four years ago, I could read the writing on the wall and prepare a contingency plan if I were not to make it to my fortyish anniversary year of employment at Allied United Insurance Company.

As I lay in my bed looking up at the ceiling, I smile to myself, thinking how prepared I am after all these years of waiting.

I am a sincere and honest individual, and if they had not made me redundant, I would not have executed my backup 'retirement plan,' but old man Nichols left me no choice. Over the past twenty-four years, I have been creating bogus life insurance policies for non-existing individuals all over Australia. These policies are of a small monetary value, something that most claim processors try to rush through in a hurry because, if you think of it, $50,000.00 does not go very far these days. All the remaining salaried claim processors are under the gun, to do a lot and thus these small claims do not get the attention they deserve.

With this in mind, I am sure the programmers of the new system will place some algorithms in the AI to expedite any claim under a particular dollar amount, just as its human predecessors did.

Twenty-four years of creating false individuals with annual payments credited into the accounting system, but no real funds received and each life insurance policy is ranging from $35,000 to the highest of $65,000 all paid for each after year. This pattern continues year after year, with each year having four policies created or a whole ninety-six policies for a sum value of $4,840,000, give or take a few thousand dollars. I call that an excellent retirement nest egg.

So this morning I will do my usual routine of having a shower and having my breakfast. But instead of going to the bus stop I will sit in front of my small DELL laptop and execute ninety-six death certificates that resemble an uncanny resemblance to the ones issued by the NSW Registry of Births, Death and Marriages and start the claims process.

The Allied Insurance Company new AI will confirm that each policy is up to date and that all the death certificates accompanied the claim form and execute payment to the designated bank on the claim form, in this case, ninety-six different accounts in multiple banking institutions in the Cayman and Nives Islands. These banks have instructions to wire any funds received on the same day to a coded Swiss bank account who have instructions to send any funds received to a digital bank in Singapore which will convert said funds into Bitcoin currency, making these funds available to me worldwide.

Finish with my typing I pack a small suitcase, made sure my passport was in my pocket and I take an Uber to the Sydney International Airport and boarded a plane to Mexico City with a transfer to the island nation of Saint Monique where a specific general will facilitate permanent citizenship for a generous payment.

In the end, the Allied United Insurance Company provided me with a retirement plan, after all.

SALAD DAYS

O ver the years, I have so many names associated with me, which made my life a living hell.

Let's see; The most memorable are 'Chubby,' 'Fat Butt,' 'Porky,' and my favourite; 'Fatso.' But those days are gone as I embarked on my new mission to lose weight today. Call my mission: Salad Days.

Salad days are great. The aim is to reduce my weight by going to a pure salad day routine every day.

That meant that for breakfast, I would indulge in a fruit salad. Lunch would comprise a mixed salad, while for dinner I would sparkle in an avocado salad.

Days went by, turning into weeks and weeks into months, and every day was a salad day. After six months, I stood in front of my digital scale and heroically I face the scale, knowing that I have triumphed over my weight issue since I faithfully adhere to my said regime, day after day after day.

I gingerly stand on the scale, barely moving a muscle since I did not want one gram of weight to shift against me during this memorable moment in my life. And the digital numbers flash as I step on the scale.

After a minute, the lights stop flickering and I look down at the registered weight; I see I gained 1 ½ kilos!

So much for salad days.

Onward to steak days!

SCIENCE FICTION WRITERS OF THE FUTURE

Have you ever wondered how science fiction writers get their ideas? I have, and I did some research that found the source of their inspiration. Friday, August 30, 1946, was an important date in history. Mars would be close to 96% full, orbiting the Sun at a distance of 1.58 AU and be at 2.28 AU from Earth. This alignment was perfect, for it allows for the first of what were to become many time travel conventions.

Meeting in the generational home of the Barleys of Happy Valley, New South Wales were distinguished science fiction writers. Let me name you a few, just their surnames since I am sure you would say these are recognisable.

Let me start with Wells, Burroughs, Asimov, Bradbury, Clarke, Heinlein, Le Guin, Butler, Dick, Orwell, and Vonnegut, to name a few of the forty attendees.

My great grandfather, Bebington Bartley, built the estate for the family home in 1830 and the estate has been in the family ever since. Granddad was a bit of an eccentric man, always dabbling in scientific experiments that sometimes would scare the living daylights of his neighbours, requiring a visit from the local constabulary to ensure safety for the community. Granddad always thought that the most thought-provoking thing that humanity possessed was time, so he set about learning as much as he could about the subject.

From his basic study of horology, which involves the measurement of time and the making of clocks, he covered everything known. Then he hit it; the ability to time travel, a simple watch that contained a mechanism that speeded time to the speed of light, or close to 300,000 kilometres per hour. Granddad was so excited that he thought he would call in the representatives of the state's newspapers; the *Colonist*, the *Australasian Chronicle*, the *Australian Call*, among others, but right before he was going to send a message for their reporters to come to the house, he changed his mind.

Not calling in the reporters was a brilliant move; the announcement of time travel would have caused mass panic in 1835, and it could have damaged the space and time continuum. Granddad then thought of the best way to use this newfound ability; he would gather as many of the most excellent science fiction writers ever born, or yet to be born, and invite them for an annual time travel convention where they could exchange thoughts, ideas, and postulations without being called many names.

The next meeting is today, Thursday, August 30[th,] 2125, and as we gather again to continue this tradition, I wonder how many potential new science fiction writers might be out there. There is a local Happy Valley community writing group fermenting talented writers of the future. Who knows?

SECOND VERSE SAME AS THE FIRST

L ove can easily break the heart. I know; it occurred to me. When I was very young, I experience puppy love, and as I grew up, I then muddle through crushes in high school and then as I achieve that young age of twenty-something, I find my real first love, and I then lose it.

We were too young to understand the intricateness of relationships, of dealing with the opposite sex in meaningful ways, so our signals were mixed and misunderstood. So, we broke up last September at what was then our favourite restaurant, Luigi's Pizzeria, just as the National Football League was starting its season. A coincidence you may say, maybe or maybe not. I cannot say for sure.

Yes, I enjoy watching my favourite team play, but my heart remembers Wilma. So, the football season came and went, the Super Bowl takes place in Tempe, Arizona, and I watch it on the TV alone. To shake off this malaise, I decide to have a treat and decide that next Thursday night dinner at Luigi's Pizzeria would do me fine. I know she will not be there.

Luigi's was close by, an easy ten-minute walk from my apartment, and I often passed it on the way home from working late and knew that Thursday night was a slow night so there would be plenty of solitude for me. I could enjoy Luigi's veal cutlets with prosciutto and sage, for Luigi's chef had an excellent way with veal.

As I enter Luigi's I find the place almost spartan which was good for me and the maitre d' points to a table which was next to an empty table on one side and a second one has a man sitting in it, and when I sat down, I could see his face and we just looked at each other. Two lonely souls, I thought to myself.

The maitre d' gives me the large menu and I raise it to inspect the offerings, but I knew that the veal cutlets with prosciutto and sage were the way to go. The chef's veal or saltimbocca, literally meaning 'jumps in the mouth,' is one of his most classic Roman dishes and he does it to perfection. The thin veal cutlets topped with slices of prosciutto and fresh sage leaves, all secured with a toothpick and then pan-fried in butter, with a quick roux sauce made by whisking a bit of flour, white wine and a lemon juice mixture and then gently stir in the same butter. My experience has been that you can wait to have this delicate dish presented to you in less than twenty minutes and I have a little white wine either from the regions of Frascati or Colli Romani, depending on the going price for the bottle.

Having given my order to the maitre d', I look around the restaurant and notice that a woman has sat at the table with the man I had seen earlier. She had her back to me, but I could hear their mutual soft words of an argument being exchanged between them like a game of tennis with each volley returned more vicious than the previous one.

Oh well, it was none of my business, so I wait for the server to bring me my bottle of wine, the San Marco Frascati Superiore, which I had selected. Made with fresh Granny Smith apples and a subtle grapey undertone followed by distinct floral tones, the wine will be light on the palate with a lovely textured feel and a balance between soft fruit and crisp acidity, a perfect fit for my upcoming feast.

As I wait for the main meal to arrive, the couple's conversation kept getting more heated, still in an undertone way, but you could feel that at any moment an eruption was going to occur.

My meal arrives, and if I had a Facebook account, I will probably be one of those that would put up a photo of the veal in all its glory with the glaze on the top and the sauce just waiting to be soaked up with crusty bread. I am not sure why this delicacy is called saltimbocca but most likely is because it is so delicious or maybe because it is so quick to make—perhaps is both! All I know that it might have taken twenty minutes to make, but in less than ten minutes I was done, and so it seemed the couple next to me.

The woman stands up quickly, grabs her water glass and splashes it in the man's face to which he gets up, looks at her with eyes that were throwing daggers and storms out of the restaurant leaving the woman, who slumps in her chair, softly sobbing.

A few minutes pass she seems to compose herself and signals for the server who arrives with the bill in which she places an Alexander Hamilton and gets up and leaves.

As she arrives at the front door, she gathers her shawl from the cloakroom; turns to place it on her shoulder and our eyes meet.

Wilma!

She stands there and continues to look at me. I sit at my table and also have my eyes centred on her. It seems an eternity, but I stand up and with my open right palm extended, I point to the empty chair at my table and motion to Wilma to sit next to me. Why I did this, I do not know. It felt right though, as I waited for her to react.

After a moment, Wilma turns, opens the door, and leaves the restaurant.

Oh well, I had a splendid meal. Did you expect a happy ending?

SISTER KATE

My high school years were the happiest of time for me. The emergence of adulthood was clear during these junior years as testosterone and ache were running rampant through my body, and it always seemed to explode at the most unfortunate of times.

At sixteen, I owned my first car, what you would call today, a vintage 1957 Chevrolet Nomad. I called it my Midnight Nomad; this classic wagon was as close to perfection as you could get. Everything in this masterpiece was new, and all metalwork and custom engine cover was done with loving hands. Front and rear bumpers were tucked, and they welded everything, unlike the plastic cars of today. A full leather interior made you think you were on a sofa while the 357-horsepower engine with "four on the floor" manual transmission gave you that "coolness" you get when driving a "stick". They bore the engine out to 405, giving it so much power that is just starting the vehicle accounted for one less litre in the fuel tank. My Midnight Nomad did not have any of the fancy extras and extra weight you have in today's cars: no power front seats, no power windows, no air conditioning, no custom stereo with an MP3 player or "Bluetooth." No FM stations, just your standard AM stations. If you drove this car, you knew you were a man.

Trying to prove how much of a man I was, I got challenged to run a couple of "doughnuts" on the practice football field and, of course, I accepted the challenge. Little did I know it was a setup and after doing the "doughnuts' on a Friday afternoon, I got called into the principal's office on Monday morning upon my arrival at the school.

Again, being a man, I accepted my responsibility for my actions, and the principal was so impressed with my grit and honesty that he gave me a month of detention after school in Sister Kate's classroom.

Sister Kate was a waste of womanhood.

From day one of my detention, she asked me to sit in the front desk, right in front of her, so no matter what I did, I always had her face in front of me, and what a face it was.

You always see those women that have not only a fascinating face, but a beautiful face. Well, Sister Kate had them all beat, without trouble. Her round face surround by the headdress made for such a beautiful framing that I was just intoxicated by her and all I could do is stare and stare at her face, and those deep blue eyes she has.

On a couple of occasions, she caught me, and I glance down at my writing book or a book just to pretend I had not been looking, but she knew I was staring at her.

Days past and they turn into weeks and then during the last week of detention during one of my "staring moments" as I became to describe them Sister Kates looks at me and says: "What are you looking at and what are you thinking?"

I do not know what possessed me to answer. I should have stayed quiet for no virtuous deeds ever go unpunished, but I blurted out: "I just thought as I watch you, Sister Kate, what could have possessed such a beautiful woman to become a nun?"

Without hesitation, she stands and points her finger at me and yells: "Young man, one more month of detention and this time with Coach Murdock."

The next month was not as pleasant since Coach Murdock coached football, but I feel justified in the uttering of my statement to Sister Kate since later on, I found out that at the end of the school year she had left the religious order and married our principal, Father Martin. So, my testosterone was not the only one running rampant that year.

THE DEFENDERS

The *Steam Room* is on a side alley behind the local chemist store off Main Street Happy Valley. They do not display its location since the Defenders took over government back in 2126 in a hostile takeover of the elected government. With the Defenders came a list of new guidelines and regulations. Because of these repressions, the establishment of the *Steam Room* and many others like it occur.

The year 2126 started like every other year. A slow period in society because of the holiday season taking hold of the communities around the country. It was during this 'slow period' that the Defenders took over by mobilising their embedded members in all chapters of government, society, and religion. Late January 25, 2126, the call went out to all Defenders to take control of all councils, hospitals and significant buildings and all power stations and water resources. In a blink of the eye, the elected democratic forces no longer exist, and the new era of the Defenders began.

By the winter of 2126, the Defenders had corralled all known proprietors of pubs, cafes, and restaurants. All Reserve Services Leagues buildings are no longer in use and all private clubs such as tennis clubs, netball clubs, golf clubs and country clubs. Add to the list all rugby clubs, soccer clubs, gridiron clubs, and any baseball and softball clubs that might have.

The Defenders did not stop their eagerness for monitoring 'controlled substances' so they set their sights on certain importers who the Defenders perceived were importing said 'controlled substances.' Importers were also incarcerated and taken to 'rehabilitation centres' for proper Defender ideology instruction. There was no area of society that the Defenders did not touch with their radical new ideology. The Defenders and their rules and regulations singled churches, mosques, synagogues, temples,

monasteries, convents, any building where a 'controlled substance' could be prepared and shared out.

A brave ex Gloria Jean's Coffee House employee by the name of Walter Killebrew decided in November 2126 that resistance needed to be formed and started in the *Steam Room* under the guise of a dry-cleaner specialising in Defender's uniforms.

Opening the *Steam Room* right under the noses of the Defenders was nothing short of both brilliant and brave. The Defenders would come by every day, dropping off and picking up their uniforms and never suspect that the *Stream Room* was a front for an illegal coffee shop.

The Defenders thought that caffeine has created most of the troubles in the world. Wars, conflicts, fights, anger; all because of the increase hyperactivity that caffeine creates or that the lack of caffeine can create, such as a depressive mood.

Walter came up with code words for his clients to identify themselves and be allowed through the back door of the dry-cleaning store. Walter adapted terms from the 1920s helping his clients and to avoid the Defenders. Terms like a *blind pig, bluenose, burning with a blue flame, coffin varnish*, were common. The phrase *hit on all sixes* became synonymous for great coffee, and Walter had many more that soon became its unique language around Happy Valley providing its citizens with a chance for a shot of coffee, albeit illegal, but coffee that stirred the memories of many.

The Defender's reign of terror lasted until 2194, when valiant descendants who were customers of the *Steam Room* said enough is enough and a counter-revolution took place on December 1st of that year and reason once again prevailed over Australia.

In less than a week, the Defenders were out of power and all its supporters stripped of their authority. Australia could now start enjoying a cup of coffee or tea without the fear of the Defenders.

So, as you take your next tea or coffee break, think of Walter Killebrew and the good he has done for Australia in the year 2194.

SLANG

Blind pig–a speakeasy or other establishment where illicit alcohol was served.
Bluenose–someone who is prudish, puritanical, or uptight.
Burning with a blue flame–drunk
Coffin Varnish - homemade liquor
Hit on all sixes - to perform at full-capacity or nail it one hundred percent

THE HAMMER OF THOR

My first train ride was at the tender age of fourteen when my father dragged me kicking and screaming on the old *Wolverine'* from Chicago, Illinois to Pontiac, Michigan to visit my grandparents.

Laying on my bench seat, I search for anything to do to relieve the boredom in my head, but I had packed nothing worthwhile that would prove to be a remedy. Sitting next to me was my old man, reading the paper, and my mother tagged along on this glorious trip.

Leaving Chicago's Union station was a slow process, but in less than ten minutes I was peering out the window at the barren lake Michigan; all frozen, devoid of life, just waiting for the early thaw of spring to flow again. My thoughts turn to my mother, and I realise what an exceptional mother she is, always there for me, no matter what. Like the time when I got into a street fight with the local bully, Johnny Butler.

It all started in a kind of innocent moment with a small comment from me, just three minor questions in a row:

'What's up, man?' 'How's it going? What is happening?' I asked.

That is all I asked and then came Johnny with: 'What did you say?'

I repeated my three questions for a second time.

Before you knew it, Johnny pounces on me as he always does, but this time, as if providence itself assisted me. Somehow, I trip Johnny, and onto the ground, he falls.

My opportunity to pounce back on him opens up, and I am straddling him with my knees on his chest, knowing that now will be the first time that I will win a fight with Johnny.

Peering into his frightened eyes, I raise my right arm, form the hardest fist with my right hand as if I held the hammer of Thor and I as I bring my fist down, a hand appears out of nowhere, grabs my arm and pulls me off Johnny's chest.

My mother had seen what was happening and fearing that I would, as always, come second in the fight, take victory away from me. All I could do was cry. Not of fear, but out of anger at my mother for negating the one moment in my life in which I was to be victorious by beating Johnny Butler to a pulp.

Thinking back on this episode of my life, I am thankful she was there, because I do not know how far I would have gone that day in punishing Johnny Butler. I could have hurt him badly since I had years of beatings inflicted on me and now was my chance for sweet revenge, but alas, it was not.

Imagine if Johnny had just answered my three questions with:

'Not much man!' 'I'm all good. Bored as hell.'

THE OBLIVIOUS WRITER

The afterlife sucks if you are a ghost. If at the time you die you have some unsettled business on Earth and you are not sure what that business is, well, you become a ghost. That prospect can be a miserable proposition, so I decided I needed to join the Sad Ghost Club (SGC). The SGC is a club for any ghost who's ever felt sad or lost. So, I joined. At my first meeting, someone asked me what I had for breakfast, which I thought was an unhappy question to ask so early in the morning, but I named all my favourite cereals that I consume at breakfast time. They include Booboo Pops, Mourn Flakes, Sulky Charms. Rice Crabbies, Frosted Mini-Weeps, Cinnamon Life Sucks, Quaker Oh Whatever's, Boo-Hoo Berry. Saddened Wheat. Honey Bunches of Oh God Why Me, Cryin' Oat Bran, Wailful Crisp, and my favourite of them all: They Lied About Me Being Special K.

A lot of the other ghosts also enjoyed these same cereals for breakfast and that got us talking and, the conversation turned out not to be very much engaging since the gist of everyone's vocalisation was to complain, whine and overall bad mouth all the living folks around us.

Modern humans are not afraid of ghosts anymore, not like in the good old days, the Victorian era. Now that was the good old days. Ghost writing writers knew how to pen about us and present us in a decent light to all their readers.

Take just four of them: Robert Louis Stevenson's, *The Body Snatcher*, Oscar Wilde's, *The Centerville Ghost*, Charles Dickens's, *The Signal-Man* and my favourite of them all: Sheridan Le Fanu's, *'An Account of Some Strange Disturbances in Aungier Street'*. Now these stories would scare the pants out of anyone, but today, nothing.

These are the days of movies like *'Ghost'* when a sexy Patrick Swayze portrays a ghost. How can I compete with that!

So alas, there is nothing for me to do but to 'officially' resign as a ghost and go into the light, but there lies the problem. I have no light to follow. Nada, zilch, zero. So, what are my alternatives to cross over.

I thought I hire some today's mediums. Folks like John Edward, Tyler Henry, or the best, Allison DuBois. Maybe if I 'knock' on their door, they might just be able to guide me to the other side. How hard can it be?

Well, I checked out Edwards and Henry, and they fizzled out. Not enough money in it for them. DuBois was at first hopeful to help but when she found out, I have not been a victim of foul play, well that cut my chance.

My enrolment in the SGC will have to continue until such a time when someone on Earth can help me cross over by instructing me on how to go into the light.

So, if you believe you might help me, just call out my name: The Oblivious Writer!

THE OUTWORLDERS

For the past six months, I have worked hard in organising, coordinating, and setting up the Happy Valley Winter Music Festival (HVSF) in the Happy Valley Showgrounds. Everything is in place, with sponsors signing on, a request for artist participants has gone out, and a lot of local talent has responded and have booked. A few prominent international artists have also signed up bringing the CWSF a pretty good worldwide notice.

The festival has attracted a pot-pourri of different music styles to please everyone attending. From art-punk, classical choral, to acid techno and Christian acid rock. I have been able to collect many groups so that the festival will be a tremendous success; and yet, I feel I am short with the repertoire that I am offering. As if my request for music has gone short; like it is missing something.

Concert day arrives, and the ticket sales were so great for the Happy Valley Showgrounds is packed with visitors waiting for the show to start. You can feel the electricity in the air from the faces of the backstage musicians and the crowd outside. Molly Cauldron, the master of ceremony, gets set to introduce the first act. As Molly steps to the stage, the crowd goes wild with anticipation of his first words to start the faithful.

Molly announces the first group; The Flying Serpents who start a melody of Afro-punk that gets the crowd swinging to the wild gyrations of the lead singer; Peter Serpent. Then comes a rendition of Mexican pop by Sarita and the Peppers, which gets the multitude again into a hot and sweaty dancing mood.

The show continues to flow with more acts of distinct variations; Turkish pop; neo-soul; reggae in Spanish; death metal and so on. The crowd is enjoying themselves, but I sense a lowering of intensity in them as if they are getting bored. I could not afford to fail in my execution of the HVMF; my reputation will be demolished, and I would be bankrupt.

As time progress, I could see small pockets of attendees slowly migrating to the exit doors showing a lack of interest in their faces. They have seen it all before. The same sounds of doo-wop; Bongo Flava; rock-and-roll; polka; Celtic folk and Manila sounds. I was losing the crowd and my future.

Suddenly, a roar is heard from above, and what I can only describe as a 'flying saucer' appears and begins descending. The crowd steps back to allow the spacecraft room to land. An opening in the craft appears, and six multi-pedal creatures disembark carrying what seems to be instruments. They propel themselves onto the stage and play the most harmonious music you ever heard, and then stop waiting to be introduced.

I rush onto the stage and grab the microphone from Molly; I scream out: 'Welcome to the Outworlders.' The crowd goes wild, and the Happy Valley Winter Music Festival will now be not world famous but universally famous.

THE PASSAGE OF VENUS

Growing up and working in a family business is always a challenge. How did it happen? What prompted your ancestors to go into this line of work? As Joe Romano is finishing his busboy duties in the restaurant, he decides it was time to ask his father that question. 'Hey dad, why did great-great-grandad decide to settle in Happy Valley in the 1880s?', ask young Joe, as he sits down next to his father on one of the dining room chairs after the restaurant closes for the evening. 'Why did he come to Australia for anyway?', ask enthusiastically young Joe, eager to have his father answer. Putting his sales receipts for the evening down and taking a sip of his Toschi limoncello Joe's dad decides maybe he should answer the question with the story his own grandfather told him of Joe's great-great-grand's arrival in Australia and settling in Happy Valley.

'Well, son, my father told me this story when I was old as you are, and I do not see any reason not to share it with you? It all started in December 1882 when the two contenders for the NSW elections for Happy Valley NSW, Mr. Thomas Gordon and Mr. Arthur Wesley were walking by the C. B. C. Bank building and speaking to their contemporaries about the upcoming elections and were each of the candidates stand on the issues,' Joe's father starting his story.

Joe's dad continues the story stating that his father told him that two gentlemen were walking down Argyle Street and they met more and more individuals, a very young man comes up to them and asks them: 'Will you support the telescope being erected on Hills Street for tonight's passage of Venus?'.

'Of what matter are you speaking of Sir?', asks Mr. Gordon.

'The passage of Venus which will occur tomorrow early morning at 01:49 AM to 06:26 AM which will provide an opportunity for improved measurements and observations of its passage,', excitingly explains the young man.

'Who are you Sir?', ask Mr. Webley.

'Scusami, my name is Pietro Romano and I am leading one of the many expeditions sent out to observe the transit from locations around the globe and we have selected this beautiful location has been selected as one of the many locations for this marvellous sight.'

'How many expeditions have been set up?' asked Mr. Webley.

'Well, Signori, there are five official French expeditions. They have dispersed one to New Zealand's Campbell Island, another to Île Saint-Paul in the Indian Ocean, while the third went to Nouméa in New Caledonia in the Pacific. The fourth travels to Nagasaki in Japan and the last one to Peking in China. In addition, there are three official British expeditions travelling to the Kerguelen Archipelago in the far southern reaches of the Indian Ocean. We will station another one to Mauritius while the last is near Cairo in Egypt.', responds Pietro, catching his breath.

'Also, the Americans are also taking part in four expeditions funded by Congress. The first one is going to Hobart, Tasmania, another one to Queenstown, New Zealand. The third is headed to Chatham Island in the southern Pacific and the last one to Vladivostok in Russia. They have instructed me to set up in this beautiful area of the country,' concludes a smiling Pietro.

'And who is to pay for the setting up of this telescope?' ask Mr. Webley.

'I was told that the Happy Valley Council would pay for the setup, have you not heard?'

Both Gordon and Webley look at each other and, as if by political instinct, they quickly answer at the same time: 'No, the Council is not paying!'

'But I have it here on paper,' says Pietro and shows the document to both gentlemen. Immediately, both of them laugh and slapping each other in the back. 'What so funny Signori?', asks a dumbfounded Pietro.

Mr. Gordon stops laughing, catches his breath and responds; 'Well, it seems you mistook Happy Valley NSW for Cowra NSW. Cowra is about sixty hours away from here and this is where your letter allows you to set up your telescope, not in Happy Valley,', again laughing.

'But if I do not setup here for passaging Venus, I will miss it and the next passage of Venus will not be available to be seen again until one hundred and twenty-two years from today or in the year 2004. I am ruined. I will be the laughingstock of the Italian Spectroscopy Society. What am I to do?', a despair young Pietro asks.

'Well, you could always stay in Happy Valley and live here,' responds Mr. Webley.

A sombre Pietro thought hard and decided that the humiliation of returning to Italy would be too much to bear and instead started the first Italian restaurant in Happy Valley appropriately named: 'Il Passaggio di Venere'.

Joe's dad stops and lets the story sink in and waits for a response. 'Oh, I see. That is why we are now in the restaurant franchise business, right, Dad?' Joe's dad looks across the table, over his son's shoulder, and rests his eyes on the framed sequential photos of Venus passing through the sun and points to the pictures. 'Yes, son, that is why the Il Passaggio di Venere #1 is the oldest restaurant in Happy Valley out of this entire chain of eateries'

Joe sits and looks pensive for a few moments and then he gets up and tells his father; 'To think I could have been an astronomer instead of a busboy. Way to go great-great-grandad!'

THE POWER OF INSIGHT

It arrived, Prom Night! The one night of the year that I worked so hard for all year long. Not only is it prom night, but I turn eighteen today. But it gets better. Bobby O'Shea, the football team's captain, says: 'You are coming to the prom with me!'

All day Saturday I was in a mess; nervous and anxious by my little brother, who kept sneaking into my room and moving my makeup kit from one side of the room to the other.

As I sit at our dining table for lunch, I cannot eat. My stomach is full of butterflies. My mother senses this; she smiles, looks at me and says: 'Child, we all have gone through this. I went through it with your father. Relax. It is just a dance.'

But I cannot relax.

No one in my family knows. My mother, my father, my little brother, and even Bobby O'Shea are unaware that I have something even more important than the prom tonight. Tonight, I get to try my superpowers!

My parents thought they could not conceive a child, so eighteen years ago they adopted me from the local orphanage and like it happens on so many an occasion when a couple cannot conceive, they adopt, relax and bam! Nine years later, my little brother appears in the picture. I am not worried I love my little brother even though for the last two years he has become a thorn in my side, but I still love him.

My thoughts are only on Bobby.

Did he ask me to the prom because he likes me?

Did he ask me out because he loves me?

Oh, I know what I feel about him, but I am also cautious because my mother always said men are flaky. They are not sure of what they want, but I can use one of my superpowers, a woman's insight. The ability to see through the murky parts of a young heart and see its true intentions and I will.

We arrive at the dance hall, and the prom has started. I see the multitude of young hearts is gathering for this perfect evening. Bobby lets go of my arm and goes and high fives a couple of his mates from the football team and there he stays for over an hour while I sit alone, just watching and waiting.

It did not take long for me to realise that I must take the initiative, so I stand up from my sitting spot, grab Bobby's hand and ask him to step outside.

There under a cloudless sky and with the light of the silvery moon with Bobby looking into my eyes, I say 'I love you, Bobby O'Shea!' Bobby laughs at me, so I step back from him; punch him in the nose, turn and walk away. Well, at least I got to use another of my powers.

34

THE RIGHT LIFE PARTNER IN TINDER

It is always so hard to find the right life partner. You look for sure signs that will give you that assurance that she is the one for you. I know what to look for in my perfect partner, and I had a mental checklist to make sure all the T's are crossed, and I's are dotted.

Of course, love plays a part in selecting your life partner, but we all must admit that physical attraction is the first thing that happens. It is the survival of the species that many times brings a man and a woman together. Sometimes it works, sometimes it does not.

In my case, I should have seen the signs.

My meeting with Matilda was purely by accident in the coffee shop next to work. I bumped into her and spilled my cup over her dress. I apologised profusely and offered to pay for her dry cleaning, and of course, we exchanged names and phone numbers.

One thing led to another, and soon our conversations were more frequent and our 'coffee breaks' coincided with each other's schedule, then lunches and then the dinners, and then we began sharing our intimate feelings and hopes.

My last few relationships failed because I was not honest with the woman I was dating, and I vow not to make this mistake with Matilda, so I was up front and honest from the moment we decided to 'take it to the next level' of this relationship.

I warned Matilda that I was not trying to shock her but that I was into S & M, that I would ask her to bring protection, that I would insist that she be on top and Matilda just sat there nodding, smiling, and saying that she understood and would be open to all of those conditions. We agree that this upcoming weekend would be the ideal time for us to 'step up' into our relationship and met at her place.

Saturday night I am all excited thinking that consummation of the most intimate moment of a couple's life would happen to us tonight. I knock on Matilda's door; she opens it and lets me into her apartment.

Matilda shows me her dining room table, all layout for tonight's dinner; spaghetti and meatballs then she shows me her new shin guards and welder's mask, and, in the bedroom, I see a bunk bed.

Well, I left Matilda's apartment thinking how could she believe that S & M was spaghetti and meatballs. Protection meant the chin guards and welder's mask and being on top meant a bunk bed.

Then I remember Matilda was a blonde.

Maybe I will try Tinder next time. I mean, how bad could it be to find my life partner there?

THE SHORTEST DAY

The evening seemed like a blur now, vanishing as a mist with little to show for other than a tremendous headache gained by my excessive drinking celebrating my new promotion to vice president of personal lending at International Commerce Bank.

Laying on my bed, I search for my phone as if it would relieve the pounding in my head, but I know I needed to check the time for of all days, today is not a day I wanted to be late for my first meeting in my new position. I worked hard for this promotion. Put in the hours and be known. I stab a few of my colleagues in the back, but such is life, right? Whatever it takes, and today I reap the rewards of my actions. Finding the phone, I look at the time and see that the digital numbers show I am way into the afternoon: 330 PM. How could have this happen?

Last night at Mick's I gather with a few of my colleagues from work to celebrate, had a nice dinner and again finish the evening with a few more drinks as more and more salutes, and raised glasses were hoisted during the evening. At no point in the night did I worry about drinking too much, for I know I can hold my drinks, but there was something different about last night. The drinks kept coming; The food was excellent as it is always at Mick's and my colleagues, well they are my friends, right?

As the cloud lifts in my mind, I remember the last hoisting of glasses. Someone suggests we finish at my place for the last round and someone else volunteers to bring the additional liquor, so why is it I cannot remember anything else after that?

The only thing I can think of is that someone put in a drug in my last drink. But why? I swing over the bed and the world spins around me. I sense my feet touching the bedroom carpet, but I cannot feel my toes as total numbness has taken over my legs. I rise and fall back on the bed, stung with the grogginess in my head. Another attempt proves successful for I am standing but standing and I walk to the toilet and see myself in the mirror and the reflection I see is a shock. Someone has gone and shaved my hair off!

Well, not shaven off but performed a surgical shave here and there making it one of the most horrific haircuts ever and I am supposed to go to my first meeting as vice president of personal lending today at 11 AM. Oh, no! I glance at my phone again at 3:53 PM. My alarm did not go off; My secretary did not call me to see why I was not there for my meeting. What in the world is going on?

As I look at my reflection, I see that there is nothing else I can do but to get out the shaving cream, the blade, and do a self-shave of my head. I am never done this so as I inflict various nicks here and there; I see the small spots of blood left behind as the blade goes in a little too deep. I finish and get into my shower. The warm water feels great and improves my outlook. Stepping out of the shower, I glance at the mirror reflection and see a new me — completely devoid of facial hair and now bald. Different, but not too shabby, I thought. As I rush to get my suit on, I glance at the phone and note the time: 420 PM. I might make it to the office before 5 PM and try to find out what has happened no sense in calling for who would believe me?

Reaching for my car keys, I head off and find the tyres of my car deflated–all four of them. So, it is no doubt that someone did not want me to make my meeting and took all the measurements. I hail an Uber, and at 5 PM, I reach the International Commerce Bank building, and I see the droves of humanity, leaving the offices after completing a day of work, whereas I had just arrived. Walking into my office, glancing at my secretary's empty desk, I slump into my chair and can only wonder how this could have been not only the worst day of my life but also the shortest day of my life.

THE HAPPY VALLEY AGENCY FOR TIME TRAVEL

'Please come in. Have a seat. May I get you an Evian?'

'There are you comfortable?'

'Need anything else?'

'Fine, let us start.'

'Welcome and allow me to introduce myself and how our agency serves its clients'.

'My name is Seiren Costa-Nichols, and I am the sole proprietor of the Happy Valley Agency for Time Travel or HATT.' 'Allow me to give you some background information on the Agency.'

'HATT is a full-service travel agency and tour operator that can assist you with all your past travel needs. Our specialty is organising and ensuring a once in a lifetime tour to any of your lesser-known instances you might not know of throughout your personal history.'

'We pride ourselves on outstanding customer service.'

'Our primary goal is to help you see your past and how it has influenced your life. We take into consideration the impact our tours have in your past; present and future timeline and we help you fulfil your overall travel experience safeguarding you as you travel to the past.'

'Our agency is a member of the Australian Space and Time Association (ASTA), and I also serve on the boards of our local RSPCA office and the local chamber of commerce in Happy Valley, NSW.'

'Questions so far?'

'Excellent, let me continue.'

'As you know, we are in the beautiful Happy Valley CBD in the Paragon Arcade, between the delicatessen and the crystal shop. I cater to an affluent clientele that wants to experience a unique travel experience, but you know that already.'

'Our services allow a client to go back up to 100-years, or less if preferred, to the point of excursion through the time-space continuum to a location and time of his/her choosing to experience a family event such as, for example, the birth of your father or mother, or a historical happening, say the bombing of Darwin during WWII.'

'We have a price list for my services, but I do not want to be so crass as to discuss the prices here. The adage applies, if you must ask, you cannot afford it.'

'The travel agency is part of my inheritance once my mother passed away. She received it from her mother. My grandmother inherited from her mother, who received it as part of her inheritance from her mother. For at least one hundred-generations to the time of Cronus, God of Time, gave the gift to my first ancestor, Athanasia. I see you nodding, and yes, I suppose I will pass on to my eldest when my end of my time on this Earth comes.'

'I will let you know referrals are our preferred mode of operation. We do not have or allow walk-ins, nor do we advertise on Facebook, Instagram. We do not even have a website.'

'Once the referred client contacts us, we must make a thorough financial assessment procedure for payment, then a meeting is set up to discuss the client's wants, and requirements and the client signs a confidentiality and liability agreement.'

'Think of it a little like the current the billionaire's club of going into space. You are pre-booking, but your adventure is much more exciting, I believe.'

'The process is quite simple for the client but a bit more challenging for the agency, hence our price list. The client decides on the travel option.'

'Here are our travel options.'

'Once you have decided on your travel option, you need to decide what day/date you wish your excursion to take place in. Now your next step is to decide on the day/date/year you wish to come into our office for the excursion.'

'Our office is a quite common-looking office with a reception area, a costume room, a documentation room, a medical room, a dressing room with this own toilet and shower, and the excursion room.'

'Once you have made the final selection of the date/day/year you will visit, our work begins. In the costume room, the design of the period's attire is made to ensure you blend into the period. Then the documentation room springs into action with all the documentation required for the era and all monies of the period.'

'In addition, we will provide you with letters of credit, passports, cash, coins, ID cards or introduction letters, anything that you may need to satisfy any curiosity raised by an official representative of the times you are visiting. We pride ourselves on being ready for all situations.'

'The medical room is self-explanatory. You do not want to send a client to an era where there is a rampant illness without proper medication. So, we will have for you all preventive shots or capsules to make sure they help withstand any disease of that time period.'

'You will go into the dressing room to put on the customer of the era or if you are taking the extended travel option, you will also get a suitcase of different customers for the various eras you are visiting. Here any makeup is applied (if applicable for the era) or if you prefer to do it yourself, you may do them yourself when you arrive at your time destination. Now you are ready for the excursion room.'

'When you enter the room, you will walk into an elegant room with many vases of different aromatic flowers, incense, soft music from the era you have selected to go back to and you will see the clear, acrylic booth where you will step into and go on to your personalised adventure.' 'I will hand you this form which you will take with you to ensure you are fully aware of everything that will happen.'

'Please take a moment to read them now.'

THE HAPPY VALLEY AGENCY FOR TIME TRAVEL LAST
INSTRUCTIONS

1. Client must wear the tracker wrist band at all times otherwise; Client cannot return to his/her current timeline.
2. The wrist band is more than a wrist band/tracker; it will monitor the conversations and actions to ensure Client does not interfere or influence the family member, friend, or historical figure Client will be observing.
3. We remind the client not to change the historical event Client is witnessing since any change may impact Client's return to his/her current timeline and.
4. Once the Client steps into the booth, a small beacon is provided for him/her to place in the same spot of arrival so the Client may find their way back to the exact spot for retrieval.
5. We will give the Client one more final warning/reminder of the Client's signed confidentiality and liability agreement, which state that any attempt to influence the past will mean HATT will erase immediately any instances the Client might have created. Client will be then banished to the timeline period he/she has selected to visit; his beacon will be remotely decommissioned and HATT will eliminate all evidence of Client's existence in his/her current timeline.
6. When it is time for the Client to return to his/her present timeline, the Client must show up at the same stop where the beacon was left, and he/she is to press the symbol on the wristband, thus enabling the Client to return to his/her current timeline.

'Well, that is all that it is to it.'

'Quite simple for you and now that I have explained our background, our fees, and what adventures are available, can you tell me when are you interested in booking an excursion?'

TOOTHPICKS

Intimacy, some folks thrive in it, others cannot seem to be comfortable in it, they seem scared of it, of letting someone in.

I sit on my bar stool in my local pub and the thought of intimacy just pops into my mind. Poof, just like that, the silly thought of how a human being can be on opposite extremes of such a feeling. It is a wonder what a couple of schooners will do to your little grey cells!

I, for one, have never been afraid of sharing my intimate feelings or thoughts. I shared them with my parents, my siblings, my relatives, my friends, and my girlfriend, and I feel good about that fact.

My schooner seems to get dry, so I finish the last sip, raise it to the barkeep and then I pick up these two toothpicks from the little glass on the bar holding hundreds of them, like a small pool of humanity.

While I wait for my nice cold schooner to arrive, I twirl the two toothpicks around the bar and bench in front of me. They look, as they twirl, like two dancers, and the more I twirl them, the more they seem to dance and not any dance, for they are dancing the most passionate of dances, the tango.

The tango is a dance that has influences from African, Native American, and European culture. Dances such as the candombe ceremonies of former slave peoples from Uruguay, which helped shape the modern-day tango. From the lower-class districts of Buenos Aires and Montevideo to the bar of my local pub, my two little toothpicks are dancing this marvellous dance.

The little toothpicks continue to twirl and twirl and as they cross each other, like the legs of the actual tango dancers, they seem to merge into one, one mind, one soul.

The two toothpicks now played the intimacy of this tango right in front of me and as I visualise this sensual dance, with two toothpicks, my mind wonders; What will my mind conjure up when my new schooner arrives?

GENUINE FRIENDSHIP

Established in 1873, the Happy Valley High School for Girls is the oldest girls' school in New South Wales. The school brings young women from all areas of Sydney into its fold. Achievements cover academic, sporting, cultural, and creative areas, with many at the national or international level. The school has excellent resources, and today it is at the forefront of technology initiatives with an extensive network system providing access to electronic resources. The school places a very high focus on ensuring quality learning and providing opportunities for gifted girls. The school culture is one of the high expectations, where students are safe to take intellectual risks within a very supportive and caring environment.

My name is Denise, and I was very fortunate to be in the graduating class of 1968. A solid group of thirty-one women graduated that warm spring day in October 1968; all had hopes for a great and prosperous life. My friends and I were no exception.

During those growing years, I had four friends that were the closest to me; Alice, a bright, and cheerful young woman that loved English. Georgia, a tiny girl but of firm opinion who always was out in front of any protest march she could find and support but still finding time for her music. Phillipa came from a wealthy family but never flaunted her wealth and was very gracious of her time with all of her classmates and was passionate about her painting.

Then there was Marley.

Marley was well unique. She never cracked a book. Marley never studied for an exam. She never paid attention in class, but when called upon, she knew the answer to the question, no matter what grade she was in. Science, English, mathematics, or languages when a teacher called on Marley, she always knew the answers. Everyone envy her for this success and ability, and when she was asked how she could recognise the answer, she took it in stride, always saying: 'It just comes to me.'

For the next fifty years, we all drifted in and out of our lives finding each other when we need a supporting friend through illness, a birth of a child, a divorce, or a death in the family. Seldom were the five of us ever together. There were always a couple of us intertwined at that moment in time. Someone would drift away because of family issues or something, and another member of our little consortium would pop up and take over her place. Marley, never connected with us since high school but we always received a Christmas card and a birthday card on each of our birthdays as if to tell us she is still with us. But never the five of us together again until tonight.

Tonight, we are gathering in a large conference room of the Sydney Hilton for our fifty-year class reunion, and twenty-five members of the graduating class have responded that they will attend including Alice, Georgia, Phillipa, Marley, and I. It will make the first time we would all be together after fifty years of separation.

We prepared the ballroom with three large circular tables, each capable of holding ten individuals, which worked out great since I was part of the organising committee. I made sure the five of us sat together so we could reminisce and share our stories.

The festivities started at 6 PM, and it was so delightful to see so many of the girls from high school, even the ones that I had not been close to. Some of them I shared classes with, or we were part of the gymnastics team and memories are what they are; we forget the terrible moments and concentrate on the good, so everyone was having a great time.

My four comrades looked terrific.

Alice is now a little plumper, well she had four beautiful children and now six grandchildren, so time takes its tolls. Georgia still looked like the revolutionary as she had been in high school. Having never married, we heard she had many lovers over the years, though; she was the same. Phillipa stood among us a goddess. She looked beautiful in her long gown, sparkling with so many diamonds; earrings, necklace, bracelet, rings that you would think South Africa mines no longer have any diamonds left. I look OK or so I thought. My life had given me a husband, two children, divorce the bastard after he had an affair with his secretary, and that divorce had made me lose so much weight that I had looked as if I had anorexia nervosa. On the positive side, once I recover from the depression, I gain some weight back, but not so much that my 68 kilos were shapely enough for me to still get a glance or two from men as I passed by.

Then there was Marley.

It was as if time had not passed. Marley looks the same and yet she looks so different in a pantsuit like an outfit that I would often see influential women CEOs of companies wear. All smart, all bright, all ready to take on the world. She looked the part.

We share more drinks as the evening progressed and then our conversations turned to more intimate aspects of our lives.

'Well Georgia, any more protest marches for us to join, petitions to sign?' asks Alice.

Laughing Georgia says, 'No Alice, getting a bit too old for the marches, but I love those online Facebook petitions, though. How about you? Any more grandchildren down the road?' Georgia muses.

'Goodness no. I cannot babysit anymore. Bob and I are just planning holidays after holidays to avoid any more babysitting duties.' Says Alice.

'By the way Phillipa, you look beautiful as you always did back in high school. What have you been up to?' Asks Alice.

'I have been so busy in so many charity events ever since Paul passed away, and with neither a child nor grandchildren, that is all I have been concentrating on keeping busy. I hate staying for too long in that big house.' States Phillipa.

Phillipa turns to me to ask me something but looks at Marley and says: 'We heard very little from you over the years other than the Christmas and birthday cards. I always thought you got angry at us for some unknown reason and wanted nothing to do with us. We at least tried to catch up with each other, but you never did. Why Marley?'

Marley sets her martini down; takes a moment to collect her thoughts and out of the blue says: 'Tomorrow, at your specialist appointment Phillipa, you will be told that you have stage III of cancer, meaning your cancer is larger and has grown into nearby tissues or lymph nodes. You will not accept this from your doctor telling her she is wrong. You are going to be given several medications which will make you tired and sick. You will purchase them and not take them and in a little over a year, you will go into stage IV and then a little later, pass away in your enormous mansion, all alone except for your maid and butler.' States Marley as she picks up her martini and takes a sip.

Silence on the table as we all digest what Marley said.

'What the hell Marley. That is an awful thing to say to Phillipa. Who gives you the right to tell such horrible lies?' I scream at Marley.

The others express several other similar sentiments to Marley, who sits there sipping her martini.

Then Phillipa speaks: 'How could you know I am going to the specialist to get results of several tests she has performed on me tomorrow? How could you know? I have not told a soul of my illnesses.' Phillipa says.

Marley continues: 'Tomorrow Alice, after thirty-one years of marriage, Bob is going to take you to your favourite restaurant and tell you he is leaving you and that he no longer loves you.'

Then looking at Georgia, Marley endures: 'Georgia, your Facebook page concerning the mistreatment of sheep exporting to the middle east will be dropped from Facebook because of pressures from middle eastern interests and local industries. Also, representatives of the ATO will show up at your home with a warrant to search your premises for illegal donations that have paid for all the ads you have placed on Facebook and other periodicals around the country.'

Marley turns to me and says: 'And you, Denise, my best friend. As you walk to the office after getting off the train at Central Station will bump into George Franklin, a man you have never met or known in your life, but that bump causes him to lose control, and he takes out a pistol and fires four shots into you point blank, killing you.'

We all sit staring at Marley, sip her martini before she stops and speaks: 'You see my dear friends; all these years, you wonder why I was always ready for answers in school, no matter what subject it was. Now that fifty years have passed, you see me as a successful woman, which I am, more successful than you can even imagine. I have done all of this for one minor reason alone. One reason I will now share with you,'

Marley continues: 'My mother shared with me her secret and lost her ability, and that became my secret. From the age of ten, I have been able to foresee the future. Not far into the future, just twenty-four hours. That is how I knew the questions to tests in advance, and I was ready with the answers. That is how I knew I was going to get called on in a class by the teacher and was ready with my answer. That is why today, I am one of the richest women in the world with financial interests worldwide and that is why I am here tonight for our fifty-year high school reunion.' 'These years I stay away from you because I knew that if I got close to any of you, I could see what your future would be in the next twenty-four hours. I could not bear the thought that something was going to happen to you, your relationship, or your family. I could not bring myself not to tell you and if I did, then tell you everything would change. Everything would change; your lives and mine, stopping this gift, this curse when I told you, so I stayed away until today.'

'Sitting here I saw your future, tomorrow's future, for each of you and I could not stomach it any longer, so I told each of you what I know, to warm you, to save you from what is going to happen. I know that from the moment I share this information, my ability will stop. I no longer will foresee the future, not even a minute ahead, but all these terrible things are going to happen to you, and I just wanted to let you know. I am so very sorry.'

Marley got up, but Phillipa grabbed her arm and said: 'Please sit Marley stay with us a little while longer.' Marley sat down with a few tears in her eyes and said: 'I am so sorry I kept away all these years. I could not bear to lose any of you when we were in high school. I kept in touch on my way. I pried from afar into your lives. I had detectives bring me photos of each of you at different stages in your lives. I felt like a stalker, but I needed to have you in my life without the fear that my ability would tell me something that was going to hurt you and, in my selfishness, I would not, and I would lose you, or someone would lose someone in their family. I am so selfish about doing what I did. I am very sorry for what I have done.' Stated Marley collapsing into the chair sobbing.

We all got up and surrounded Marley and just waited for her to stop sobbing. A few glances from the other tables and a few of the other girls attempted to come over to see what was happening, but we stopped them.

A few minutes passed, and Alice said: 'OK, we know what Marley said, it all makes sense now, so how are we going to change our future, tomorrow's future now?'

'Well, I for one I am going to go home pack, destroy all the files and hard drives I have at home and I am on the next airplane in the morning to Armenia, I have relatives there, and I should be OK.' Says Georgia.

'After we finish this event tonight, I am going home to Bob, and we are having the first of many one on one deep conversation. I am not losing the man I love without a fight. He may not love me, but I have enough love for the two of us. I have a lot invested in this marriage and will not lose it,' pounces Alice.

Phillipa looks at Marley and declares: 'Tomorrow when the doctor tells me my condition, explains the drugs and medications and procedures that I am about to undergo, I will follow them to the letter of the word. I also want to make sure that all of you are well taken care of in the event something goes wrong, and I die. I will have my lawyers draft a new will, leaving all of you my wealth, but the most important thing is I will make sure I know where each of you is every day of my life. I will not die in my big house with only my maid and butler by my side.'

It was my turn, and I was so glad I had the most straightforward solution of all. I said: 'I will not go to work tomorrow. I will call in a sickie so no train ride, no Central Station, no bumping into George Franklin, thus no death!' I said.

It was Marley's turn, and we watched her speak a little differently than ever before she said: 'For the first time in over half a century, I do not know what tomorrow will bring. I am relieved. What time is it?' Marley said.

It was a few minutes after midnight and tomorrow was here, and we all had something significant to do.

It is seldom that anyone has time to change their future and that a friend is there to help you through it, but we did. We helped each other once more, just like we have always done in high school.

That is genuine friendship.

WEREWOLVES OF HAPPY VALLEY

The hands were pale grey as if the circulation had long stopped, and the ring upon the finger of the right hand seemed to glow with a spark of inner fire. Stripping small pieces of meat, the left hand brings the morsels of meat into a mouth great and full, with the sharpest and cruel teeth of a beast. Slowing down its chewing, the creature yawns and lays down on the ground. Sleep is what it needs.

'Wake up, Billy, wake up!' says Amelia, his little sister.

Billy opens his eyes and sees his little sister standing over him, looking shaken and scared. He feels cold and notices that he has no clothes on and realises that he must have transformed. Damn it, Billy thinks to himself, I hate it when and Amelia finds me in this state.

'It is OK Amelia. I am OK. A bit tired and cold, please hand me my clothes' says Billy.

Amelia looks around and finds a pile of clothes placed beside an old tree stump, picks them up and hands them to Billy and turns around as not to see his nakedness. Billy puts on his clothes and, using his right hand, combs his hair as best as possible.

'Come on, Amelia, let's walk home. It is almost time for breakfast.' Billy states.

Amelia had found Billy close to the edge of the Nepean River in the Rotary Cowpasture Reserve in Happy Valley, New South Wales. This area is a mixture of different environments. There is a baseball field, a track run and many scenic bushland areas where different species of birds and animals have their habitats. The reserve is an area where plenty of activity occurs during the day, but it is empty at night. This is the reason Billy comes here at night to transform, to prey, to hunt, to kill!

'Oh Billy, why don't you tell Mum what is happening?' exclaims Amelia.

'Amelia, Mum would not understand. She did not even know that our father could transform. How do you expect her to understand that only the male descendants of Lycaon have this transformation curse?' Billy answers.

His father, rest his soul, explained everything to him at the young age of twelve. Billy, like his father and his grandfather, was progenies of Lycaon, who had angered the god Zeus when Lycaon served Zeus a meal made from the remains of a sacrificed boy. As punishment, the enraged Zeus turned Lycaon and his sons into wolves and thus the curse began, centuries ago.

The night of the first full moon after Billy's eighteen birthday, Billy had his first transformation. Billy was prepared. His father had explained what he needed to do for the first transformation and for the subsequent changes to come until his last day on Earth. The knowledge of what was to happen did not make it any better for Billy. He feared what he was transforming into and the urge that drove him to prey, to hunt and to kill. Amelia was ten when Billy went through his first transformation and a better sister he could not have. She had found him near the first spot where he had his transformation as agreed upon and had made sure he got home. Now fourteen Amelia had a brother in his mid-twenties that if people found out that he was a werewolf, he would be captured, prodded, poked and experimented upon to find the source of this power but she knew there was no power, only a curse.

As Billy and Amelia walk up Argyle Street heading toward Landana Avenue to the safety of their home, they see the posters on some trees and poles asking for information as to the recent killing of platypus, magpies, and plovers and even some snakes, all found torn to pieces as if eaten by a fierce animal. Billy and Amelia did not stop to look at the posters; they knew and did not relish the thought of seeing the photos or information on the posted flyers.

As they near their home, Amelia asks; 'Billy, will it ever stop, this curse?'

'No, it will only stop when I died, and I will make sure the curse stops with me, for I will attempt never to marry and have a male child because if I do, the curse will continue,' answers Billy

'Then I will also not marry, and the curse will stop with me as well.' Says Amelia.

A big smile comes over Billy's face; 'Amelia, only the males' offspring of Lycaon are cursed, not the females. You will have a wonderful life filled with love, children, and family, of this, I am sure.'

As Amelia opens the front gate to their home, the front door opens, and their mother comes out: 'Where have you two been to so early in the morning?' Their mother asks.

'Billy and I went for an early morning walk around Happy Valley to enjoy those early morning sounds before the roar of the cars take over the morning. It is always so beautiful and tranquil down by the reserve and during our walk back,' Amelia finished.

'You two are so much like your father. He always used to do the same every month like clockwork, rest his soul. Now go freshen up and get ready for breakfast before you both get to school and work.' Said the mother.

Billy and Amelia look at each, smile and head upstairs to freshen up for breakfast and get ready for their respective day. They hear their mother turn on the radio to the oldie station in Happy Valley and Warren Zevon's song blares out.

Aa-hooo! Werewolves of London!
Aa-hooo!
Aa-hooo! Werewolves of London!
Aa-hooo!

I am sure you could sing that song here in Happy Valley, just the same, thought Billy, but who would believe it.

WHAT IF HE SAID YES

She might never get the chance to be alone with him again. Her husband was across the country; he'd never find out, so why not? It has been sixteen years since she saw him last. It was at their high school graduation and she remembers him like it was yesterday.

Her parents never liked him, and she did not understand why. He was always polite to her, always willing to help with any homework assignments, and he even volunteers in the church every summer doing odd jobs.

Still, nothing he did was acceptable to her parents.

If you meet him for the first time, you find him plain, even common. Not a tall young man, average size, thick black hair, and he wore the ugliest pair of glasses you could ever see. It made his face look like one of those 1920s headlights, but his smile. That got you.

His smile was always present. It seems he never had a bad day, and he always made sure you also had a great day. He had crooked teeth his parents could not afford expensive orthodontics, but it did not matter to her. All she saw were those two small specks of eyes behind the glasses that gleam like grey pearls in the ocean's bottom.

Now sixteen years later he walks into her life and she feels compelled to throw all inhibition out the door and start a moment of illicit affection with a man she has not seen in many years.

She knows she might not have that chance again and her window of opportunity is open for just a few days, so she decided that is now or never, in for a penny, in for a pound. She gets up and walks over to the table where he is sitting, pulls up a chair and sits and just looks into his eyes.

He is not wearing those hideous glasses. Were they hideous in high school? She wonders, but still, he looks as interesting and charming as she remembers him. He speaks. He recognises her, but she holds her hand up and instead offers to him a proposition, a proposition that she would have never thought of if he had not walked into this bar.

He listens to her as she explains what she has wanted for so many years. What dreams she had. What thoughts had been in her heart all these years. He listens and does not speak but offers that smile that reassures her he is relishing everything she is saying to him.

She finishes and just stares at him, hoping that her proposition did not put him off. He looks at her with those grey eyes of his and smiles and says: 'Your husband may not know but I would know' and gets up from the table and leaving her to wonder - what if he had said yes!

WHAT WAS WRITTEN ON THE SIGN INTO THE BEAR PARK?

The moment I left my car and wandered into the lush forest; I knew I should have paid attention to the bear sign. At the start of my trek as I wandered deeper into the woods, I tried to remember what the sign said, about the points about the grizzly bears.

My memory is sharp, and I remember there were at least nine bullet points on the sign, making it easier to remember. If I recall some bullet points dealt with: First, fresh tracks. It is often better to see the bear's tracks than to see the actual bear. If you can tell the direction that the bear is travelling in, it is prudent to change your course of direction. Bears will travel down the same pathways as people or other large animals use. Checked!

Second, scat. Bear scat will look different depending on the bear's diet. Close examination of bear scat can sometimes give you a sign of what the bears have been eating for a year. If the scat contains remnants of human garbage, there is a human food conditioned bear in the area. Checked my backpack, compass, matches, poncho and only water, good.

Third, animal carcasses. I remember this one a lot because it said in bold letters. IF YOU COME ACROSS A CARCASS, LEAVE THE AREA IMMEDIATELY.

Fourth, torn-up logs and stumps. Bears will forage for insects in dead logs and rotting trees. Got it. Avoid this as well.

Fifth, evidence of any digging. Bears, especially grizzly bears, dig holes on the ground as they search for roots or ground squirrels. Grizzlies will dig for food in the early spring when they first leave their dens. Noted in my mind.

Sixth bullet point, claw marks on trees. If you see claw marks on trees, it means the bear has climbed that tree and around. Be sure to look up and not scream. Noted.

Seventh, if you find hair on trees. Bears will rub against trees, trees with rough bark, to scratch themselves. Also, I need to remember that the higher the hair left on the tree, the bigger the bear. That YouTube video of the bear scratching himself pops to mind. Noted. A big one!

Eighth daybeds. Bears love to be most active in the early morning and in the evening. During the heat of the day, bears will rest in daybeds. These are shallow depressions of piled up leaves in the forest, trampled vegetation, a shallow scrape, or a hole. Daybeds are in cool places. Bears will make daybeds along streams and rivers. Daybeds are often associated with feeding places and therefore should be avoided.

Ninth, what was that last bullet point?

I stop by this nice little creek and look at my watch; 9:10 AM. The morning is still nice and cool, and the sun has not stung yet. The running water gives a constant rumbling sound, and it surrounds me the longer I stand there. I look in the water's direction flow and see that there is nothing in the creek that may have precipitated an increase in the water flow but the rumbling is getting louder and louder so I decide to turn and go on with my trek when I see the large grizzly standing behind me and I recall the last bullet point as I see this gigantic paw being raised at me............

.

WHO DOES ANYWAY?

Tuesday is my grocery day. I am not sure how Tuesday became my grocery day, but it just did. I guess it happens like many things in life occur. You get into a routine, and each day of the week, you select something that may need to get done around the house. You know, the little things, like sweeping the floor, vacuuming, dusting, doing laundry and on and on. So, Tuesday became my grocery day.

As I park my car along Main Street in Happy Valley, New South Wales, I thank divine intervention for I was fortunate to find one of the few four-hour free parking spots and I scooted my little Fiat into it.

Getting out of the car, I unlock the boot and get my grocery bags since the local grocery has joined the masses of retail stores now banning plastic bags, so everyone must remember to bring their own. I extract about four sacks or five bags. I can not tell since they are inside each other. Close the boots and, using my remote control, I press the button and the 'beep-beep' sound of security rings in my ears.

I turn to walk and slam into a woman standing right behind me.

'Hi, Angus,' said the woman.

'Sorry, but do I know you?' I asked since I had never seen this person before in my life.

'Of course, you do, Angus. I am God.'

OK, I know I heard the woman say, 'I am God.' So, I know I am awake and not having a dream. I can see myself in the reflection of Bert's Barber Shop and see the same reflection of the woman. She is in her early thirties, attractive, with hazel eyes and an olive skin tone. Standing tall, her height is the first thing you notice and then yes, her deep yet adorable eyes, which are significant but sad looking. She is wearing a fabulous, pocketed short dress with a hand-drawn print of Parisian ladies enjoying a rainy day around the city with their dogs paired with crisp lapels, front buttons, and a self-sash to sweeten up her looks. Add to this the highest high heels I have ever seen a woman wear, and I thought that for God, she looked great, of course.

'OK, I have heard a lot of pickup lines, but I have to admit that this is one of the best and I have ever heard. This pickup line glows!' I said, smiling at the woman.

'Well, I am not trying to pick you up, Angus. I thought that because you had such a terrible weekend that maybe I come down and make sure you got one of the primo parking spots on Main Street, so here I was saving it for you.' 'God,' said.

Well, I have to admit I remember driving past Bert's shop and not seeing this spot and then going around the round-about and as if by magic, the spot was here. Maybe I missed it. Just a coincidence, I thought.

'I could classify finding a parking spot on Main Street as the miracle of the day, but it was just my lucky day today. Besides, why would 'God' even waste his time on something so trivial.' I answered.

'First Angus, it is not He but She, as you can see as I am standing in front of you and you are not due to wear glasses until your forty-four birthday which is only eight years from now so I take your statement to be just a macho statement. Second, there has always been a misunderstanding by humanity that I am a male but as you can see, I am a female.' Answered 'God.'

'So, in the Bible when it says that God created Man and then when he was lonely, God created Woman, that is wrong?' I blurted out as I stood in front of Bert's shop.

'Angus, I created Woman first, which goes without saying in my image. Then seeing she was lonely, I noted I made a mistake and to make up for it I created Man not the way they printed it in all those books.' Answered 'God.'

Ah, here we go I think; 'OK, what gives lady? If you are 'God', how could you even make a mistake in the first place? I asked, feeling good about myself.

'Well, Angus, it was not a mistake for a formulation error. When I created Woman, I made sure that there was plenty of dopamine in her chemistry and I also ensure that it included both norepinephrine and phenylethylamine and a pinch of oxytocin for good measure. This mixture was just right, I thought, but it was missing something.' Explained God.

'Yeah, it was missing, Man. You still have not answered the question of how the Bible has the story wrong?' I pushed 'God,' to explain.

'Patience Angus, I am getting there. When I saw Woman, I saw she was missing testosterone, so I created Man and gave him plenty of the stuff. I thought that was it, a perfect match, but I did not see it at that moment.' said 'God.'

'Angus, I thought these chemicals had to be in Woman and Man, but that was not right. Dopamine, testosterone, oxytocin, norepinephrine and phenylethylamine all work together to create a better human being. It is how much of each that makes a difference, why Men are Men and Women are Women, sort of speak. The chemistry worked itself out at the end with Women becoming more alert with their feelings and social skills while Men, driving by their higher levels of testosterone, to push themselves forward to bigger things. It's not a theory nor is it a fact, it just works like that most of the time and all these chemicals allow Woman and Man to love, cuddle and procreate the Earth.' said 'God.'

'I still do not have my answer God!' again I exclaim, this time a bit more assertive than before.

God smiles, and she says; 'my point, Angus. All these chemicals have made Women more patient than Men, and that is why I was here today to help you find a parking spot. To answer your Bible question, the reason the Bible version you have today is the way it is today and not the other way around is that................'

The shirking alarm clock is screaming out to me, telling me it is 7 AM and time to get up. I hit the off button and check and see that it is the 5th, a Tuesday, my grocery day. I get up and perform those daily routines everyone does in the morning, shave, shower, have breakfast and get ready to do my daily runs. Oh yes, it is Tuesday, so I do my groceries today.

I get in my car and drive to Main Street to see if there is one of those few four-hour free parking stops there for me, and as I drive past Bert's Barber Shop, I noticed that there is none.

Oh hell, I guess I will have to drive six blocks down a side street to find a parking spot. I do not have the patience to look for one on Main Street. Who does anyway?

CAN YOU NOTICE?

Around this time of the year, I get that mushy feeling. A feeling that lets me know that summer has passed. Autumn is around the corner, and I am ready for it. All around me, I see the leaves falling from the trees, like snowflakes at Thredbo. Usually, my wife and I argue a little. 'I am getting cold sweetie, turn on the heater,' she says. 'Absolutely not,' I answer. 'Use a jumper to keep you warmer,' I cheerfully say to her.

Now you would say that I was a 'meanie' to my wife doing this. Nay, I would say, for I must think of the bills that come during the prelude months of winter. You know, the heating bills that skyrocket out of this world since our utility bills are one of the highest in the country. I succumbed to the insistence of my bride and turn up the heating dial. Not much, just a degree or two enough for her to feel the warmth cascade on her as she sits in front of the television and watches 'Doctor, Doctor' and drool at Rodger Corser.

I know you; the reader might have noticed a theme here.

Have you?

Usually easy to spot, and I wonder if you have this time.

Tell me what it is!

If the reader cannot figure it out, please email me at info@northportbooksellers.com.au for the answer.

BRING IT ON!

Last night Martha made me my favourite dinner, steak with string beans and almonds, mashed sweet potatoes and my most favourite of all desserts, cherry pie.

I topped the evening off with a glass of wine. The evening was nice and warm, with breezes blowing in through the open windows. There is nothing like a New York night to calm your spirits. I would go to bed early since I had a strenuous day.

Morning arrived, and I did not see Martha, so I assume she had awakened earlier to make breakfast. Suddenly there is a tremendous racket downstairs and I run and find Martha standing in the kitchen with an unusual box speaking to her with people inside!

I am having a dream; I am sure of it; I think to myself. But as I see Martha standing there trembling, I see that is it reality. Martha is holding a newspaper and hands it to me. Her face is numb. I glance at it and the first thing I see is the date–October 17, 2024.

'Martha, is this a prank, my dear? Are your brothers trying to rile you up this morning or, me?'

'No George. Look outside. The world we knew is gone. There is a strange world out there.'

I walk over to the kitchen window and indeed see a vastly different world. A strange world. It has to be a dream; I say to myself; it just has to!

Suddenly there is a knock at the front door of the house, and I do not see my servant, so still holding the newspaper I open the door myself with a mental note to reprimand James when next I see him. Opening the door, I find a half-naked woman standing in front of me with a stick with some soft covering over it. she immediately speaks.

'Mr Washington, what do you think of President's Crumble tweet last night? Are you in favour or against this proposition? How are you going to counteract the tweet?' she asks.

'My dear lady, first you must cover your legs, for I can see your knees it is quite improper for a lady to be seen in such attire. Second, what do you mean by a 'tweet' and who is President Crumble?' I stop to hand the lady a shawl I retrieved from the coat hanger next to the front door.

Without skipping a moment, the young lady shows me the most curious little box which she easily handles in her small hand, and it has a small piece of glass and in its letters is printed on it. The letters say: 'Washington has no chance of winning the nomination this year. I have all the votes. Let him try.'

Standing at my doorstep I am having a conversation with a strange woman who is speaking to me about someone called Crumble who believes he can win, what I am not sure of winning what, but insisted in very few words, that he can win.

'Young lady, pray tell, what is this little box and what is this writing on it?' I ask.

The woman looks amused and says: 'OK, I will play along. It is the latest tweet from President Crumble, who is running for re-election this November. He is saying you cannot beat him for the nomination. What do you have to say to that, Mr Washington?'

'A tweet? What are you saying, young lady? What is going on? Did my wife's brother, Bartholomew, put you up to this prank?' I felt a slow boiling anger fuel inside of me, but I knew Martha would disapprove, so I calmed myself and it was a good thing I did, for Martha just showed up at that moment.

'George dearest, who is this improperly dress young lady standing at our doorstep. Please usher her inside before the neighbours see her is such a disarray!' Grabbing the young lady's arm, Martha quickly ushers her inside into our foyer. I ask again; 'Young lady, what is your name and what in the world are you speaking about?'

'Mr and Mrs Washington, my name is Rosemary Chapel, formally from Australian Television Corporation news and current affairs division and now a reporter for Cable Network News and I am here to get your reaction to this year's Republican contest for the 2024 presidential election. President Crumble does not believe you can muster the votes to take the nomination away from him to face Biden. What do you have to add to this, Mr Washington?'

This is quite an amazing situation; I think to myself. I went to sleep in 1797 and woke up in 2024 alongside my Martha in a strange new world which is becoming stranger as the moments pass.

'Miss Chapel, I am a private citizen now having retired from the Presidency in 1797 and you tell me is now 2024. I ask again. Is this one of Martha's siblings' pranks?'

'Mr Washington, I am not sure why you keep insisting that this is a prank, sir. The country wants to know what your response to President's Crumble tweet this morning will be. Let your fellow country men and women know today. The country awaits!'

'Here, is your Twitter account, sir. What do you have to say to Crumble?'

Everything was going well until we woke up in this strange new world.

I look at Martha, who is standing there looking at me as she has always had. Proud, strong, knowing that together we can take on the world, this world. I once more look at the newspaper I held in my hand and notice a strange phrase, but I like it and decide to use it.

'Miss Chapel, would you be so kind to prepare this statement for me to President Crumble using your little box and my account, as you mentioned?'

'Sure Mr Washington. What would you like me to tweet?'

I glance at the newspaper once more, smile at Martha, and I respond. 'Bring it on!'

IT SEEMED LIKE A CLEVER IDEA AT THE TIME

Summer is a wonderful time of the year. The sun seems brighter; the air seems fresher; the birds were happier and we get to go to the pool. St. Michael's Home for Boys in Rayburn, Georgia, was an orphanage that had one hundred boys of different ages living in the home. Their parents placed all the boys in the care of the Sisters of the Valley because of assorted reasons. Some of them the boys had health and mental issues. Add to this a unique mix a group of twelve Cuban boys that were part of the 'Pedro Pan' initiative and you got yourself quite a challenge.

The 'Pedro Pan' or 'Peter Pan' initiative was a clandestine US instigated mass exodus of over 14,000 unaccompanied Cuban boys and girls ages 6 to 18 to the United States over a two-year span from 1960 to 1962. Our parents, who were alarmed by unfounded rumours circulating amongst Cuban families that the new Castro government was planning to end parental rights and place minors in communist indoctrination centres in the USSR.

They established the Catholic orphanage in 1869. When I and the rest of the Cuban boys arrived in 1962, the place looked, well, old. The orphanage had a pool, but this year the pool had been drained and other than a small puddle near the drain, no other water was to flow into it. This meant that this summer was going to be quite a bore. We asked questions to the nuns, and the answers we received were unsatisfactory. We were told excuses like; 'We cannot afford to spend money on filling the pool. You will go to Boy Scout camp this year. They will have a pool there. We are not paying for a lifeguard this year.' So, we got the gist, no pool.

It was going to be a boring summer indeed.

The pool had a large cabana with one door. Inside, there were two bench seats in each corner of the small rectangular building. Each of the small sections of the rectangle has an opening about three metres from the ground to let in light and ventilation. The opening was 900mm wide by 500mm high and it had no glass or fly screen on. It was a simply opening. No one could look inside from the outside unless you had a three-metre ladder.

Being enterprising young men and considering we were all bored out of our mind, we decided that a game of chance should take place, but it would have to be a game of chance that provided challenge, adventure, risk, and danger. It is absolutely amazing to see a young boy's mind at work.

We decided that the fairest manner in selecting a candidate for this venture was to draw straws. Having picked some straws, we cut several strands into equal sizes and we voted we could hold these pieces in one hand but one. The one size that was different was shorter than all the rest. Now we needed to have a prize. The logic was that whoever picked the shorter straw would become the candidate to win the prize.

The prize proved to be a challenge. Living in the orphanage we did not really have anything of value with us, but someone produced a brilliant idea; let's smuggled food out of the kitchen from the priest's lunch or dinner, especially desserts. This idea for a prize was splendid because the kitchen cook was an excellent baker. We agreed and at the first opportunity, a large chocolate piece of cake was smuggled out by the boy working the clean-up shift in the kitchen and hidden for this event.

Then came selecting a candidate for the challenge.

Again, the boys reasoned that a reward, such as the piece of chocolate cake, should have a fee attached to it, so we decide that a small bag of marbles with a minimum of twenty marbles in the bag would qualify you to a chance to earn a chance at the challenge and the cake reward.

Candidates poured from all corners of the home, vying for a chance at the challenge. As long as the candidates brought their bag of marbles, we did not care what nationality they were. A bag of marbles at the orphanage was like gold.

Finally, we agreed on the rules. Once an individual makes the marble bag payment, he got to pick one straw, and you hold on to it until all candidates finished drawing their own straw. Once all the straws were picked, we all would show our straw, and the boy with the smaller straw 'won' the chance to earn the cake.

Now this is where things got exciting. The chance to win the cake still came with another challenge. That challenge was to dodge the bricks, six of them to be exact. The winning candidate then went into the cabana and had to dodge the six bricks being thrown in through the two openings at any speed or time that the boy holding the brick could hurl. If the candidate did not get a scratch from the brick, he won the cake. Disqualification was simple to see. If a candidate gets hit with the brick on the arm or the hand or just a nick, he will get disqualified, then another new candidate would try to win the cake.

It was so simple, it was brilliant.

Even with this danger and risk, there was a hunger for the cake, so there was always someone willing to win the cake.

The event was a success and a lot of fun, however, that was until Michael Wayne Johnson had his chance.

Michael Wayne Johnson was not as fortunate.

On the third throw of the brick (no one actually admitted flinging the brick through the opening), it bongs him on the head, cracking his skull requiring and a ride to the emergency room and twenty-two stitches.

The nuns were stunned and furious.

They took all the participants into a classroom and there the Mother Superior and two sisters interrogated us all, one by one, in order to find the brain-master of the event. Everyone kept quiet, played dumb, and stood together in solidarity.

When it became my turn at the inquisition and they asked me why we thought this would have been a game to be played, all I said that it seemed like a clever idea.

IT WAS A SHOCKING NOISE

G rowing up in the 1970s was a blast and you could not find a more fitting place to blast away the night than Underground Atlanta. Founded in 1969, Underground Atlanta (the city beneath the streets) used the old viaducts that lay beneath the streets of downtown Atlanta to create a complex that contained over thirty restaurants, music venues, bars, and nightclubs with all of them flourishing in this unique environment amongst the old storefronts that would remain open late into the night. The original architecture was from the 1920s, which gave Underground Atlanta not only a unique feel but added to one of the greatest and most brilliant aspects of the site, which was the fact that alcohol is available in all the establishments.

These factors made Underground Atlanta a popular spot for both the locals and tourists that came into the downtown area of the city. One of the 'in spots' was Dante's Down the Hatch, which was frequented by the rich and famous and somehow, I wounded up there one night.

If memory serves me well, I wanted to impress the lady I was with that night by showing off all my moves. That evening I hoped the music to be loud and the dance floor to be packed with bodies gyrating to the 'Hustle,' the 'Bump' and many more illustrious moves from the era.

My date for the night looked stunning.

A long evening dress with a long slit in the front which allows her long right leg to show off both of her muscular and toned legs. The dress joined in the middle with a long belt like swab that separated the bottom floral aspect of the dress with a night black top that just shimmered in her long beautiful blonde hair. How I had snared this beauty was beyond me, but snare I did.

We waited outside in the long queue to gain access into Dante's and the line did not seem to move, but that did not bother me for it gave me the opportunity to carry a conversation with my date. She mentioned she had never been to Dante's and had heard nothing but wonderful things about it from her friends. I played cool and mentioned I had been here before (OK, just once) and would agree with her friends that the place was indeed the 'in spot' in Atlanta.

We continue to inch forward towards the entrance, and we could see the door bouncer, a mountain of a man, even from afar.

As we got closer, I notice my date started to not pay as much attention to my conversation, but she kept glancing towards the bouncer and I could see that he also had made eye contact with her and smiled a lot our way (her way?). I persisted in trying to ensure that the conversation was lively, interesting, and most important about her but no matter what I did, all I got was a nod, a small smile, a little giggle and the ever glance over to the bouncer.

As we arrive at the front of the line, the bouncer, in an authoritative voice, says; 'ID, buddy.' To which I produce my driver licence, which he takes looks at and return to me without taking his eyes off my date.

'ID please Miss.' Smiling mountain man asks my date.

My date reaches into her purse and attempts to find her ID to no avail and then smiles at the bouncer and with most coquetted voice you ever heard says; 'Why Sir, I seemed to have misplaced my ID. Surely you can make an exception for me?' and touches the arm of the bouncer in what I thought was a very provocative manner.

He looks at her for a moment or two, smiles and says, 'Sure. You good to come in but not you!' looking straight at me.

My date looks at me, smiles and says, 'Ciao, see you around!'

I am not sure what possessed me but at that moment she walked across the door I stomped on the train of her evening dress and then a shocking noise tears through the sound of the music blasting through the front door; the sound of the largest cloth tear you ever heard.

All I see is the back of my date's underwear and her evening dress is all over the floor and everyone, including the bouncer, is laughing at her.

My date looks at me in horror and I smiled at her. All I say to her is 'Ciao.' And as I turn and start heading home, all I seem to hear is that shocking tearing noise in my mind.

MARCH FORTH!

There is a possibility I am getting old, much older than I may want to admit. Last week at the gathering of our local writers' group, they gave the homework assignments out and for the life of me, I somehow botched them all up.

The group leader for the meeting was kind enough to detail the four different topics slowly, eloquently, and phonetically and to ensure accuracy, she even handed out a slip of paper with the topics written on them.

Still, I screwed it up.

Not only did I not hear her distinctive voice detailing and explaining the topics, but I totally messed up the written topics as well. My conclusion is that I am now losing both my hearing and my eyesight, and I direly need repair.

The meeting was on St. Patrick Day and I wore green, hoping that would enhance my chances of good luck, but that strategy failed. To top that, it was my brother's birthday, and I forgot to send him a Jib Jab card, so I guess I started a small riff in the family.

Since we met on the 17th of March, I thought I had missed the misfortunes of the ides of March, but I can now say that misfortunes carry over.

So, what am I going to do now?

I am going to march forth and keep writing and pay more attention to the next homework assignments!

MEMORIES

Sitting by the window, the memories always seem to flow back into my mind of carefree days gone but not forgotten. The beautiful woman that, for her own reasons, decided that I 'was a catch' and married me back on that Saturday 31, 1970. She thought it would be fun getting married on Halloween Day and I did not care what date, as long as I held her in my arms on that day.

She is gone now. It is now fifty years since that day and yet it is so clear in my mind. My memories.

NEXT TIME, CHEW MORE

Arriving at the restaurant for my early dinner, I acknowledged Michael, the server who has served me for the last three years and he ushered me to my favourite table, number 7, by the large front window which looks out on the street.

Today's menu brought taste sensations which I have experienced before because the special of the evening was maghaz.

Maghaz is a Pakistani curry dish containing actual brains. Sheep or cow brains, to be exact, and it is sometimes called 'Brain Masala.'

'Good evening, sir. How are we this evening?'

'We are fine, my dear Michael. Would you be so kind to once again describe to me tonight's special of maghaz and bring me the coldest Roof Afza you have?'

Smiling, for he knows me so well, Michael starts. 'The chef boils the brains first before he stirs fries them with onions, coriander seeds, green chilies, turmeric and ginger-garlic paste, and they are best served with parathas which are pan-fried flatbread,' says Michael.

There is no decision to be made since this is one of my favourite dishes. Michael receives my order and my drink order and he goes to place my order.

Ah, Roof Afza, I tried the drink once while in London on a holiday and it was delicious. 'Rooh Afza—one that enhances the spirit and uplifts the soul,' says its manufacturer, Hamdard Laboratories.

The drink is a combination of sugar, fruits, herbs, vegetables, and natural extract of citrus flower. Michael always adds basil seeds. I know these seeds to treat diabetes because they lower the sugar levels and balance the digestive system. As a result, the combination of both it should rejuvenate you and give you an enormous boost of energy.

The drink arrives and I savour it while thinking of the upcoming brain Masala and it too it arrives.

Depending on where the chef is from, i.e., Pakistani, Bangladeshi, or Indian, the cuisine is the same but different. The chef is from the Indian Punjab region, so the maghaz has that reddish, deep red, stocky look that is inviting for you to dip into with your parathas. I dipped into the plate.

It excited my sense of smell as the mixture of spices blend with the brains and sticks to the paratha and erupts when in enters my nostrils. I pick up a paratha, dip it, and bring this dish of the sub-continent into my mouth.

An explosion occurs in my brain as the blends of the spices melt into the cow's brain and I, at first, chew my meal but as the flavours continue to grow and dive, not dip, into the meal.

I dig in more rapidly, as if someone were going to take it away from me. More mouthfuls invade and I do not seem to have enough of it, and then; I choke.

I heard that when you think you are dying, your life passes in front of you as blur and you relive it. Well, I can say that when your life passes in front of you, but in my case, it was not my life but Michael's, the server.

It seems Michael is more connected to me I ever thought since glimpses of his life pass by me as I choke on my maghaz and paratha. It seems Michael has had a fun life working as a labourer, a teacher, a jazz trumpet player, and now a server. In less than ten seconds, his life passes in front of me like a movie, or so I think, as I continue to choke.

Michael swings his fist and slams my back, scaring the living daylights out of me and out comes a chuck of cow's brain, lands on the table and I can breathe again.

'Thanks Michael. I almost die!'

'That is OK, Sir. You are lucky that I once understudy for Peter Salisbury to be a professional wrestler in the WWE and still remember some things.'

Well, that was one-part of his life I did not relive.

Next time I will chew more.

SCAMS

"I am thinking about you, as usual. I want you to know how much I sincerely love the times we have had chatting on the phone. It means so much to me. It seems like I have known you forever, and I cannot envision my life without you. You know I am not looking back, I have no second thoughts, and for sure, no regrets at all. I can say that I want you and need only you, and I see our love growing stronger with time. This expression of my love for you should not frighten you. Please do not be scared, my love, for life hits you with unanticipated things that take you by surprise. I know it did for me the moment I first hear your voice over the phone. All I can say is, you are the most wonderful and best surprise that I have been so fortunate to have in my life, and you have shown me how much caring, understanding and love you can share with me that for that I thank you and I am enriched by having you in my life now, and I'll never let you go," so said the lovely young voice over the phone to me.

Around this time of the year, I get that mushy and lonely feeling that is so common at this time of the year. Yes, it is the Christmas holiday season and as a single man, I get lonely during this festive time. If are like me and have no one to share the holiday with, then the sound of this sweet voice will hook you the moment you first hear her and hook me it did.

The conversation started with the natural, 'Hello', and before I could say anything the lovely voice started into her aforementioned spiel, which I listen to knowing that this was the first time I have heard her voice. It is a lovely voice which I could listen to for as long as she continued to speak, but I knew I meant nothing to her since it was a wrong number likely or something else.

After a few more minutes, I stopped her and asked; 'Who are you?'

'Stephanie silly, I cannot believe you do not recognise my voice!'

No, I did not recognise her voice nor her name, but I said, 'Oh, yes Stephanie, yes, my mind must have drifted the moment I heard your voice, so sorry. How are you?'

'I am fine. Just thinking of you and wishing I had enough money saved up to visit you this Christmas for I miss you so much.'

'Oh, you were planning to visit me. You have not said that before. What has made you say that?' I query.

'I miss you terribly silly man and if I could afford the plane ticket of $1,834.00, I would be in your arms in a split second,'

'Is that all you need, $1,834.00? I could send you the money and when you can, you just repay me. How does that sound?' I blurted.

'That would be so nice of you!' the honeyed voice said.

'Great. Give me your banking details and I will transfer the funds as soon as we hang up.' I urgently said.

'Can you not do the funds transfer while we are on the phone that way, I can confirm receipt right away?' Stephanie said.

I answered. 'Sorry Stephanie, but I have to get to my computer and do the transfer there where it is more secured but do not worry, you will see the funds in your account in the morning for sure.'

'But if you use my Pay ID, which is my email, I can give it to you right now. The funds will be there in minutes, so I can book the plane ticket today. I just do not want to waste a day not being with you.' An eager Stephanie said in her enchanting voice.

'I cannot. I will transfer the funds via my computer to your bank details. I am sure one day will not hurt our relationship.'

Sensing I would not change my mind, Stephanie provided me with her banking details, which were a strange row of numbers not used in Australia and I finished the conversation with; 'Stephanie, my sweet. Please call me when you receive the funds so I can know your flight details to pick you up at the airport. Speak to you soon.'

As soon as I placed the phone down, I cancelled my phone number with my provider and got a new one. Sitting in my lounge, I wonder if Stephanie would find me again and try one of the nicest scams I have heard in a while.

THE AZRAEL KEY

The key in the shape of a snake laid before me, put there by the solicitor. 'There you go. That is all your late uncle Mortimer McDonald left in the will for you,' and that is all he said to me and handed me my copy of my late uncle's will. I perused it, and that is all it said. 'I leave my nephew Bartholomew McDonald, my most prized possession, the Azrael Key.'

'So, what is this key for? What does it do? Is it for his house?' I asked the solicitor.

'Yes,' he answers and leaves the room, leaving me alone with the will and the key.

Wow, I did not know what to do, so I grab the key and walked out of his office to a nearby park to ponder the meaning of this strange event. My uncle was always a quirky guy. My mother always told me that her older brother always had a 'strangeness about him,' like a cloud of doom would appear at any moment.

I always liked Uncle Mortimer. He was a lot of fun with all his stories and shenanigans he got us into in his old house. He is, was, always a blast, or so I thought. But this small key was something to think about.

First the name he gave it, the Azrael Key. The name Azrael is a boy's name of Hebrew origin meaning 'help of God'. This is also the name of the Angel of Death in Jewish and Muslim tradition, not a brilliant start for an innocent child just born into the world, so why this name and what does it mean? What does it open? With no other course, I walk to my car, start the car, and pointed it towards my late uncle's home to investigate the key. It had to do something. It had to mean something.

The old house looked like it always looked to me when I was a young boy and would visit my uncle. It has been a while since I last saw him, maybe in late 1995 and he was already in his early 70s and nothing had changed, at least on the outside that I could see. I go up the four steps onto the front porch, move the screen door, and place the Azrael key into the lock. The door opens, and a musty smell empowers my nose, and I almost gag a little. I wait a few moments until my eyes adjust to the darkness and wander in.

Starting in the lounge area, I open the window shades to let the sunshine come in and its rays hit all the little knick knacks my uncle had around the place as if bringing them to life. Just as I remember as a young lad.

I proceed throughout the house into the bedroom, the kitchen, the laundry, the guest room and then his study, here however, I encounter a problem; the door is locked. Why is this door locked? What could Uncle Mortimer have in the study that is so valuable that the door needs to be locked?

Taking the key out of my pocket, I insert it into the keyhole and I feel the key vibrate so I pull my hand away. I watch as the key turns and hear the lock tumbler click into the unlock position and the door opens. OK, now this is strange, I think to myself, taking the key out of the keyhole.

Pushing the door wide open, I find Uncle Mortimer's study stuck in time, just like the rest of the house: everything stood in place, as time never passed.

Opening the window shades, I bring light into the darkness and made for a more interesting observation. In the middle of the desk lies a metallic looking box with strange figures and symbols. As I get closer, I see the box had an opening for a key and it made sense to me that the key I held in my hand should be the key to open this box.

Placing the key in the keyhole, I sense, again, a vibration, but this time it is coming from the box. I turn the key and lift the lid and I find.........

THE BETRAYAL

Relationships are so difficult, for they require so many parameters for them to succeed. Some of these parameters are spending time together, clear communication, being playful, acceptance of the other's limitations, trust, respect, loyalty, and affection, to name a few. Over the years that I have been in my present relationship, these parameters are filled and I thought equally shared, but I was wrong.

As we walked through the park last week, our friendship is relationship examined, and it failed on so many levels, I am embarrassed to say.

A simple hello and an offering from a stranger that came up to us, and that is all it took to break the bond I thought we had.

The betrayal that I felt was huge. How could a simple gesture and offering break the many years I had invested in this relationship? How fragile was our bond, and I did not see it? How could I have been so naïve?

All these thoughts came over me as I watch Rover just lie back on his back and continue to enjoy the rubs, he was receiving from this stranger who had offered him a treat.

It will take time, but this betrayal is something I will always remember.

THE CHAIR MAN

The trip back to home to Elstone Manor was going to be a bit of a bummer. Dad died last week and now all the siblings, mother and my brother Seth and sister Abigail were heading back to Happy Valley New South Wales (NSW) for the reading of the will by Dad's solicitor, Ms Anna Willerton from the firm Creston, Robertson, Abbott, and Paulson. Oh, it was going to be a real bummer indeed.

It was a typical morning in Happy Valley NSW as the plane made its final descent into Happy Valley regional airport from Guam, where I was doing missionary work. The sun rose early this summer day as the plane was landing. I could see all of Happy Valley below me in its splendour with the cement and tile colour roofs bringing a beautiful kaleidoscope of colours to be seen from above. Beautiful, I thought, but it was still going to be a bummer of a day.

As I landed and the door of the plane was open to disembark, the heat was already pestering at 28 C. It was going to be a sweltering day today. One of dad's companies' jets got me in Hagåtña Guam's capital city, as I am sure some other companies' Dads own sent their planes and did the same for Mother, Seth, and Abigail. Dad's living siblings, Uncle Robert, and Aunty Beth, well, I am sure they had to pay to get to Happy Valley since a long time ago they and Dad had their falling out and have not spoken in years. Man, oh man, it was going to be a bummer of a day.

The drive home was quick and easy. While Happy Valley has grown in size over the past years as most of Sydney, the regional airport is close to my ancestral home and only passes by large fields of cows grazing and both the local primary and high school which I attended what now seems a long, long time ago. Looking through the limo's window, I remember a few good days in those halls of learning, but a lot of bad ones since, as most people do not know, money does not bring happiness all the time.

As the limo pulls into the driveway, I see the large monolithic building, Elstone Manor. I did not make Dad's funeral nor wake, and why should I have? Every day growing up, it reminded me that Abigail was the prettiest and my oldest brother Seth the smartest. What was I. an afterthought, I presume since Dad never bothered giving me any worthwhile attention? Yet, I loved the old bastard.

Looking back, I resented Dad for that, but as I got into high school; I saw the stress my brother had being the oldest to carry the torch, but then again; he did not give a damn; he wasted his education and time with Dad.

Abigail was as beautiful as Mother when she first met Dad based on the photos, I seen but life has a way of turning that first love into something hard, dry, and Mother and Dad drifted from each other over the years and when I was nineteen, fifteen years ago, they divorced and went their separate ways. I do not think they ever spoke to each other again.

So here we are, a dysfunctional family, as you can find coming together to share the wealth of a bitter old man who had died alone in a huge, empty, and loveless house. Dad only surrounded himself with his business colleagues and lawyers the last fifteen years, and that dedication meant that his companies grew in size, power, and prestige. Now his heirs will benefit from his arduous work.

The entire Elstone family worked for one of Dad's companies, so everyone was on the payroll. Abigail was president of Stardust Cosmetics, Seth ran Elstone Optics, Uncle Robert ran a small subsidiary in Atlanta Georgia called Cool Dips while Aunty Beth was head of marketing for the same company. Mother also works for one of dad's companies, well, sort of. As head of development in Artistic Fashions, Australia LTD Mother got to travel, have a nice expense account, a salary, and wear a lot of new fashions before they even hit the catwalks of New York, Paris, London, and Sydney.

I took another path. After college, I borrow $200,000 from Dad which I paid back in the first ten years after university by some savvy investments and decided that the world had enough capitalist and off; I went on missionary work for the past five years.

Renting my two-bedroom apartment in Pyrmont for five years was a blessing. I could pay Dad his money, at the same time my $200,000 investment quadruple when an American investment company bought the current building owner, poured $35M in upgrades and people started selling and buying units thus increasing my value and I did not have to do anything. Got to love capitalism.

All these thoughts in a few minutes before the driver opens the limo's door and I get out and walk into the hallway of Elstone Manor.

Standing in the massive hallway, I felt bummed out. There to meet me was Ms Willerton, ready to perform her duties.

'Good morning Mr. Elstone. I hope you had a pleasant trip. Would you like to freshen up before the reading of the will? Your Mother, siblings, uncle, and aunt have arrived and waiting in your late Father's office,'.

'No, I am quite right. Let's get started. The sooner we do this, the sooner I return to Guam,' I said.

Walking into Dad's office brought a rush of memories. I remember many times sitting on his lap while he read aloud contracts, cursing every so often, picking up the phone and ordering changes from the lawyers. Dad did all this with me on his lap, but he seldom looked at me. He once or twice

77

cuddled me when I ask what I now know was a silly question such as 'Dad, why do you want another phone company? Does the one you already have not worked?' Or something even sillier as the time he called me into his office and there must have been ten lawyers standing around and I started crying when I walked in. Dad immediately asked me in a loud voice: 'Joseph, why are you crying? I simply said; Dad, you always tell me you work with clowns and I walk into your office and see none.' Dad smiled at me that time, called me over and gave me one of the biggest hugs I ever received from him. As I walk into the room, I see everyone sitting in front of Dad's desk. Oh, gosh, it is really going to be a big bummer of a day.

There was only one chair empty off to the side. It was a chair my dad had made a long time ago with his bare hands and I got to work on it with him. Seth said he hates tools. Abigail was too soft and Mother, well, Mother just would not sit in such a hard chair, for it did not even have cushions. When Dad and I finished the chair, he picked it up, brought into this office, and placed it in front of his desk and there it stood for many years. Over the years, the chair got old and rickety, but Dad never moved it. I asked once why, and he said that the world be under this, my throne, one day if I look! I never thought of that statement until today.

My Dad was many things; ruthless, greedy, a punisher but never funny, so I did not get the meaning. And yet, there is the chair, so I sit in it.

Miss Willerton speaks; 'Thank you all for coming today. I will now open the will and read it aloud for all to hear.' Ms Willerton opens the large envelope, looks inside, and pulls out one sheet. She looks perplex and looks inside the large envelope, but nothing else falls out, just the one sheet.

She picks it up and starts reading; 'Today you are all here because I am dead, buried and probably forgotten already. All of you have been living from me all these years and I do not blame you I blame myself for raising such spoilt children and having a wife that I started with in an immense moment of love that slowly faded as materialistic things are given to her.'

Ms Willerton stopped for a second. You could hear a pin drop. She then continues.

'My brother Robert and sister Beth did nothing for themselves. Just hitched themselves to my success and lived the good life. Again, I do not blame you, Robert, and Beth. It was my fault for not kicking out of the business a long time ago.'

'Seth, my first born, I placed so much stress on you to prepare you for what was ahead and you failed. You failed not because I did not prepare you for you went to the best schools and spent times in all of my companies with fine managers. You failed because you did not care. You assumed that as the eldest, all would come to you.'

'Abigail, my beautiful Abigail, I failed you too. By always tending to you as a princess, you did nothing in the way of work. Even today, you are president of a company that has not grown in the past four years in sales or market share. But again, this is my fault, not yours, for I failed you.'

Again, Ms Willerton catches her breath and stops and looks around. Everyone, including me, is in a state of shock. Dad again is at his best. Arrogant, exacting and defaming and demeaning all around him. My turn had not arrived, but I expected nothing from him, so I was not worried.

Miss Willerton continues: 'To my youngest son Joseph, I owe a lot. I never really appreciated him. His warm, his laughter, his way of asking questions that brighten my day. I never told you how happy you made me.' 'You expected nothing from me and always gave me 100% of yourself. When you asked me for a loan to purchase your own place, I gave it thinking I would not see a cent back and yet all funds were reimbursed and even a small interest payment included.' 'Joseph, you surprised me when you decided that working in a comfortable job for one of your Father's companies' was not for you. You take off for the hard streets of the capital of Guam to do missionary work. You never ask for money to help with your work and yet in all that misery that you saw, you still remember my birthday and sent me a small note. They were so much cherished as I kept them all.'

Ms Willerton stops since she has a chocking moment. I have to admit I am surprised at dad's words. So, he noticed me over the years, just could not show it much. Well, that was good, for I always loved him, warts, and all, as they say.

Miss Willerton clears her throat and starts again; 'So let me get to the point everyone is waiting for. The division of all my world possessions. First, all employment positions in all my companies held by my former wife, my son Seth, daughter Abigail, brother Robert and sister Beth are to be ended immediately. All contract termination clauses will apply, and the attorney firm of Creston, Robertson, Abbott, and Paulson will disburse the sum shown in the will by the end of the day. The planes in which you arrived will return you to your homes and there waiting will be representatives of said aforementioned firm which will let you collect your belongings and you will be out of the homes by end of day.'

The commotion was unbelievable. Screams, cries at various crescendos could be heard. Profanities were flying like frisbees in a park and all directed at my late Dad. Then silence suddenly appears when Seth said: 'Wait, what about Joseph, what does he get?'

Miss Willerton says there are two paragraphs left to be read, and she reads them: 'To Joseph, I leave the old rickety chair we built together. The chair that not one of you sat in because it was an old, rickety, and worthless. The chair that I knew my youngest would see and sit in it,'.

79

'Joseph, I leave you the chair and the leadership and ownership of all my companies, all properties, all funds in bank accounts and the estate known as Elstone Manor. Put it all to effective use. Love Dad,'

The eruption was worse than the first commotion caused by the first part of the reading. Statements like: 'We will sue you, Joseph. You can't get away with this. How did you poison Dad against us? What did you tell your Dad about us? I am your Mother Joseph, surely you will take care of me?' and so forth and so on for a few more minutes.

All I could do was stand up, and all became quiet.

I reached and picked up the rickety chair my Dad and I made and walked out of the room; out of Elstone Manor, into the waiting limo and with the chair in the back seat, told the driver; 'Please take my Dad's chair and I to the airport. Call ahead to the pilot that we want to go to the Sydney headquarters for the chair, man, and I have work to do.'

THE GREAT BATTLE

The key in winning a battle is composed of many strategies and this battle was won with the knowledge of six of them: make sure your supply chain is ready, pick your battles, hit them where it hurts, overwhelm with speed and suddenness, segment your forces, and deny them a target.

It all starts rather harmlessly. Jacinto Gonzalez was playing ring marbles with Randy MacFarlane on Tuesday afternoon after school. It was a spring afternoon, so the wintry frost that hit St. Michael's Home for Boys in Rayburn, Georgia, still hardened the ground, in 1962. The red Georgia clay is always hard, but this afternoon it seemed extra hard, making it very conducive for a fast game of ring marble.

Ring marble is a very easy game to play and the rules are flaky since there seems to be many variations of the game but the overall gist of the game is to create a large circle, most of the time at least two metres in diameter, in which you place your forty-nine small marbles and your opponent does the same. It is always best played with you having one colour of marbles and your opponent another colour. Each player has a larger marble called a 'Tolley' which is used to 'push' the opponent's marbles out of the circle. Each marble that you push counts as a point. If you happen to 'push' your own marble, well, your opponent gets that point. The player, with the most marbles at the end, wins, and the best part, he gets to keep all the marbles.

A rather simple game that is learned but mastering it, well, that takes a lot of practice. My friend Jacinto was being hustled that afternoon by Randy, who had a lot of practice at this game. Before you knew it, Jacinto was down to his last ten marbles. A group of other boys friends of Randy had gathered around them and started cheering each time Randy 'pushed' a marble outside the ring and booing Jacinto when he missed a shot. This did not help Jacinto one bit, and he deteriorated and lost the game.

After his victory, Randy further humiliated Jacinto by provoking him into a fist fight, which Randy won as well due to sheer size.

Nose bleeding, bruised and demoralised Jacinto laid on the red clay for a while and when the voices of Randy and his cohorts were off in a distance Jacinto got himself up and ran toward the barn where a couple of his friends, including me, were doing some extra chores.

Jacinto was one of twelve Cuban boys living at the orphanage, courtesy of the 'Pedro Pan' initiative. The 'Pedro Pan' or 'Peter Pan' operation was a clandestine US instigated mass exodus of over 14,000 unaccompanied Cuban minors ages 6 to 18 to the United States over a two-year span from 1960 to

1962. Our parents, who were alarmed by unfounded rumours circulating amongst Cuban families sent us away thinking that the new Castro government was planning to end parental rights and place minors in communist indoctrination centres in the USSR.

Jacinto explained what had happened to us and we all listen to the story and I could see that Jacinto's friends were itching for a fight but there was a problem which they did not seem to realise three problems.

First size, Randy, and his friends were the older kids in the orphanage, so not only they carry weight and size, but muscle. Two, there were more of them than there were us (we only numbered twelve) and last, we were the 'newbies' in the orphanage and we had not had time to see if any of the other boys could become our friends, our new allies per se. We needed a plan.

Jacinto continued his lamentation, and as he continues his story, I realised how to bring Randy and his friends to a common ground: we will use the battle strategies already mentioned. We will hit them where it hurts, overwhelm them with speed and suddenness, segment our forces, pick our battle, and deny them a target. But first we needed ammunition, that is our supply chain, and I knew who could help Alberto.

Alberto was one of the smaller Cuban boys in our group, but he was a wily guy and if there was a thing, he could do it very well it was that he played a mean game of marbles. Alberto had already accumulated all the Cuban boys' marbles, including mine, but since he was much smaller than the rest of us, he did not mix with the other boys in the orphanage. This was about to change.

We developed a careful plan in which Alberto, with three other Cuban boys, would challenge another boy for a marble challenge. As expected, Alberto won. We continued this scheme until Alberto had gained all the marbles in the orphanage except for those that Randy and his friends had. We never counted them but at the end of all the games we had three full medium size pails filled with marbles all the way to the top. We had our ammunition. Next, we pick our battle.

The plan was to wait until the night prayers had concluded. The nun on the watch did her round around the dormitory and we waited until she turns off the lights. With the lights off, from under the beds we take out and place the gridiron helmets we had taken from the games room on our heads, thus providing us with much needed protection. We gather at the end of the dormitory and, as quiet as possible, start laying on their sides the mattresses, the pillows, the box springs, everything. The barricade is up, and this ensures we are not an easy target. We then segmented our forces into three groups of four, each with its own pail of marbles. Now comes the ultimate strategy.

We have given Jacinto the honour of declaring the battle is open. He stands on a box spring and yells at the top of his voice; 'War!',

With the scream we implement the ultimate strategy, overwhelm them with speed and suddenness as a flurry of marbles start flying from three different advantage points.

Randy and his friends do not know what is happening other than marbles are flying and many are hitting their targets. Heads, arms, chest, just about everybody part is an easy target because Jacinto's scream got all the boys out of their beds and, standing even in the night's shadow, they became an easy target.

Randy and his associates realised what was happening and immediately started turning their beds over for coverage and they scrambled on the floor to gather as many of the marbles to return fire.

Both sides were now firing back at each other.

Some throws went astray, hitting some boys we did not intend to fight with, but those are the casualties of war, right, collateral damage, I believe it is called. Moore marble hits landed on the pictures of saints, crucifixes, vases of flowers and windows, causing an awful mess of glass, porcelain pieces, and small chips of woods all scatter about. We did not care, for we continued letting our marbles fly and hit their targets or.

It seemed the great battle went on for ever, but it was only minutes because the lights came on and several of the nuns came running into the dormitory screaming at all of us to stop and pulling boys left and right.

With the lights on, we assessed the damage.

Several of Randy's cohorts had bumps showing on their foreheads. Some were crying, but all were in shock. The dormitory was a mess and the Mother Superior instructed the rest of the evening for Randy and his friends and the twelve Cuban boys to clean up, pick up the debris, and then we stood in silence in two rows until dawn.

It did not faze us, for two things occurred on the night of the great battle.

We earn respect and no one ever messed with Jacinto again.

THE GREAT ESCAPE

The warden walked amongst the rows of single beds, each holding the small bodies of the inmates. She twirls her beads, and the jingle makes a singular sound which is amplified in the dormitory's silence. It does not matter because I am on to her and her cohorts and how they handle themselves in the evening as their black gowns blend in with the drab grey walls of the dorm.

A headcount. They always did it at night just to be sure we were all there. No one is missing, otherwise the alarm would be raised, the lights turned on and the small inmates would be lined up in front of their small beds and counted. Not tonight. All inmates accounted for.

I had seen the routine developed over the months that I had lived at the St. Joseph Home for Boys in Rayburn, Georgia. My compatriots and I arrived here in February 1962 in the middle of winter and as much as we tried, we could not acclimate to the rigours routine the warden and her cohorts strived to instil in us.

I, along with another eleven Cuban boys, were part of the 'Pedro Pan' operation. The 'Pedro Pan' or 'Peter Pan' operation was a clandestine US instigated mass exodus of over 14,000 unaccompanied Cuban minors ages 6 to 18 to the United States over a two-year span from 1960 to 1962. Our parents, who were alarmed by unfounded rumours circulating amongst Cuban families that the new Castro government was planning to end parental rights and place minors in communist indoctrination centres in the USSR.

This operation meant that once we were placed in the orphanage, we were up at 4 AM each day in order to go to a high Mass at 5 AM for an entire hour. Then a quick breakfast, which included a slight break before classes started at 7 AM until 3 PM, when we would work and perform some of the farm duties, they had assigned us to do. Then dinner at 6 PM, study after that, and 8 PM bedtime. Then repeat. Day after day with only a slight variation on Saturday and Sunday, but always the high mass at 5 AM.

I, rather, we, were told we would live in 'a rich man's home in Rayburn, Georgia', but it turned out to be an orphanage. Lies from day one and nonstop torture, or so it seemed, to us.

As I laid in my bed and watched the shadowy figure go by, I smiled, for I knew that in the morning all would change. Tomorrow, Saturday, my compatriots and I would escape this madness. We had planned the escape as best we could with the limited resources we had. Using an old Rand-McNally map we found in an old box, we mapped out an escape from Rayburn, Georgia to the state capital, Atlanta and from there we would get to Miami, Florida and then back to our parents in La Habana, Cuba. Friday night, everyone was eager, thrilled, excited and ready to go on Saturday. I continued thinking about the great escape until I faded into my dreams for the night.

The Saturday routine did not differ. Up at 4 AM, high Mass at 5 AM, breakfast with a minor break and then morning chores with a minor break before lunch at noon. Having finished lunch and the cleaning chores, we gathered at the appointed meeting place. I was expecting twelve compatriots, including myself, but only ten showed up.

'What happen to Pedro and Miquel?' I asked.

'Sorry, they are not sure they want to come.' A sad looking Pablo said.

'OK,' I said, 'let us walk to the jump off point at the end of the property where we will not be seen. Everyone brought their stuff?' I asked and received a few nods and glum faces.

'What is wrong?' I almost screamed.

'Jose,' Alberto said, 'a few of us have been thinking that this may not be such a good idea after all. Miami is so far away, and we are going to get hungry, so Tomas, Pascual, Gilberto, Jacinto, and I wanted to let you know that we have changed our minds and wanted you to know.'

I was stunned. I felt deserted, but I knew that this was going to be a risky proposition, so it did not surprise me. 'I understand. No hard feelings.' And I nodded and motion to the rest to follow me.

We walked in silence to the jump off point the five of us–Pablo, Jaime, Daniel, Humberto, and me. I was not sure of what was going to happen when we reached the jump off point, but I knew I was determined to get to Miami and then onwards to La Habana and I hoped the rest of my countrymen felt the same.

Reaching the jump off point at the end of the property, we could see the road and I took out the map. "There, that is Georgia State Route 44. All we have to do is go west towards Atlanta. Are you ready?" I ask, folding the map and tucking it into my back pocket.

The remaining five of us just stood around in a circle for a moment until Pablo spoke up; 'Jose', I cannot do this. I am scared that the 'monjas' (nuns) will get upset and punish us more.' As he turns and starts returning towards the home. 'Anyone else?' I look around and see the faces of terrified young boys. 'OK, go, just do not tell them which way I am headed.' And the remaining group run after Pablo, leaving me along to stare at Georgia State Route 44.

As their figures look smaller in the distance, I take a big breath of air and start running west. And run I did; I must have run for over thirty minutes until I felt I had put plenty of distance in me and the home so I could relax and slow down to a walk.

Walking and looking for any type of marker that would tell me how far I had walked was difficult as I hoped, but then I saw a sign that said Union Point 20 miles. Taking out the map, I found the spot and saw that at least on the map it was close by. It elated me because looking at the map, I could see that from Union Point to Atlanta was only four inches on the map. I would be there by night fall I was sure of it.

Continuing my trek, I started consuming my supplies, an apple, a banana, and a warm can of Coca-Cola and knew I should have packed more but I was sure I would be in Union Point soon and I might ask someone for food.

It had to be hours when I saw a little sign welcoming me to Union Point and I saw a large cemetery to the left of the road and further down the Union Point Gas, Grocery, and Deli Stop. I headed there straight for even with my limited knowledge of the English language, I knew 'grocery' meant food.

The Union Point Gas, Grocery, and Deli Stop was a ridiculously small store. One gasoline pump outside, but inside it was nice and warm, so I walked up to the old man behind the counter. He asked me a lot of questions, but I kept silence and kept pointing to the bag of potato chips and cans of Coca-Cola. He got my message for the next thing I know. He grabs a couple of bags of potato chips and a can of Coca-Cola and hands them to me. I smiled and tear one bag open and start devouring the chips while taking sips of the nice, cold Coca-Cola.

Enthralled with the potato chips and the Coca-Cola, I did not notice the old man go to the rear of the store and make a call.

Finishing the second bag of potato chips and burping the last bit of Coca-Cola, I was ready to continue my journey when, through the front door, walked in the largest man I had ever seen in my life. He had to be eight feet tall, I thought, and was wearing a police officer's uniform and hat and walks straight to me and starts asking me questions.

Since the silence method worked with the old man, I thought I would do the same and point to the front door. The police officer smiled, nodded at the old man, and took my hand, which disappeared inside of his, and we went outside.

Waiting outside was the shiniest state of Georgia trooper patrol car I seen. He placed me in the front seat and we took off in the direction which I had just come from. I had been busted and my face must have revealed my disappointment, for the big state trooper smiled and pointed to a switch and told me I should push it up, which I did.

the blue lights and siren started, and I started laughing and so did the state trooper as we headed back to the home and the end of my great escape.

THE MOST UNUSUAL JOB I EVER HAD

The day started as most wintry days in Georgia do, dreary, wet, and foggy, just miserable. Having spent some of my formative years in an orphanage in Rayburn, Georgia, was an interesting time in my young life. The nuns that ran the orphanage were gentle wardens, who, mostly part, tried handling young boys with no life experiences, or so I thought.

Over one hundred boys were interned in the St. Michael's Home and most of them had some type of emotional or physical issue with them and somehow, I wound up right smack in the middle of this mess. How did I wind up here, you might ask?

The reason: communism.

The 'Pedro Pan' or 'Peter Pan' operation was a clandestine US instigated mass exodus of over 14,000 unaccompanied Cuban minors ages 6 to 18 to the United States over a two-year span from 1960 to 1962. Our parents, who were alarmed by unfounded rumours circulating amongst Cuban families that the new Castro government was planning to end parental rights and place minors in communist indoctrination centres in the USSR. But that is another story for another time. This story is about the most unusual job I ever had while at the orphanage.

Most of the boys had their regular routines.

Making our beds, cleaning the hallways, dusting, polishing the chapel's pews, washing, and drying dishes in the kitchen. Taking care of various animals at the farm; cows, sheep, bulls, chickens. You name it, we had them. All typical mundane jobs except for once a month. Once a month, we took a trip.

We liked the trip itself, mind you. We got out of the red brick mausoleum that was our home and got to see the 'outside world' which was a real treat. What we dreaded was where the bus was taking us, for we knew it was going to be awful.

Frequently we visited old peoples home to sing to them.

Other times we visited animal rescue centres and help clean the dog, cat, and bird cages and many times we did not even get to pet the puppies or kittens.

Today, we were sure it was going to be another surprise, but we knew it would not be good. It never was.

As we drove on Georgia Route 78, the misty rain continued, letting us know that the day would not go well for us. As we weaved through minor country roads and past countless farms isolated from the main road by long gravel driveways that would lead the driver to an old farmhouse or barn. They all seem deserted, devoid of life and yet, we continued driving for what seemed to us like hours, but in reality, it was only a forty-minute drive.

We then arrived at one of those gravel roads off the Route 78 and inwards we went. The bus bouncing, rattling our teeth with each bump and pothole until we arrived at what looked like an old wood chapel with a nearby cemetery.

The main nun driving the bus, Sister Francesca, takes hold of the handle and opens the door and the other nun, Sister Mary Magdalene, in the front seat, gets up and says: 'Children, we are here. Please get out of the bus.' I thought they were going to kill us and leave us in the graveyard, and so did many other of the young boys.

Once we got off the bus, Sister Mary Magdalene led us to the chapel and, taking out a key, she unlocks the door. The ancient door creaks open and we move into the chapel. Into the unknown, I thought to myself.

'Children,' Sister Mary Magdalene said, 'We are going to spend the morning cleaning up the chapel and the graveyard. Sister Francesca will take some of you to the graveyard and tell you what needs to be done there. The rest will stay here with me and clean the chapel.'

So, there we stood, twelve Cuban boys from the 'Pedro Pan' operation waiting to be picked. Twenty-four eyes darted left and right, scoping the old chapel for a way out, but there was none to be seen. We needed an escape plan, but we had none. There would be one later, but again, that is another story for another time.

The chapel was tiny, and it only had ten pews, five on each side of the chapel with the middle left open where the priest would march in to celebrate Mass. We stood like ducks in a shooting gallery waiting to be picked for either the chapel clean up or the graveyard clean up.

I crossed my fingers and hoped that the nuns would pick me for the chapel clean up.

I should have prayed because I was picked for the graveyard clean up instead.

The nuns marched six unfortunate little boys into the graveyard, each carrying a bucket full of water, sponges, and brushes led by Sister Francesca.

The graveyard was ancient.

Most of the tombstones were broken, leaning over, or almost completely crumbled down. Many had all kinds of kudzu crawling over them. The dates on most were illegible but in some you could see the dates, 'Mary Boswell — 1835-1852', 'Matthew Carmichael — 1840 -1899'.

This was a depressing place.

Some boys started sniffing a little when they started washing down the tombstones. I somehow kept it together as I approached the grave. I was to take care of; 'Walter Buchanan 1812-1850'.

The tombstone was leaning, so before I could start cleaning it, Sister Francesca said that I should straighten it up. So, I stood in front of the tombstone. I grabbed the stone with both hands and, using what I thought was herculean strength, I shifted the stone from its leaning position to an upright position.

This movement caused the earth where I was standing to sink, and I drop about a metre while still holding the stone.

I believe at that precise moment I learned how to fly for the next thing I remember I am cowering inside the bus, refusing to leave the safety of those old bus seats as Sister Francesca kept telling me to get off the bus.

Many years have passed and no job, paid or unpaid, has even come close to be as unusual as this job.

THE PHOTOGRAPH

Winter 2020, all of 2020, so far, has been quite an experience because of the COVID-19 crisis enveloping the world and our country. Because of COVID-19, I had to do a lot of changes to my daily routine, which meant I had to get used to the 'new normal' and like everyone else, I had no choice but to adjust and survive.

One of the many chores I took on was to organise old photos that had accumulated in old shoe boxes over the many years. How I never did the reasonable thing, you know, organising the photos after you have the photos developed and then you place them in your photo album with brief notes to remind you of the wonderful moments you had throughout your life. Well, I failed and to my surprise, I failed miserably since I found photos going back to the summer of 1963 and in particular an old photograph of the seven 'charioteers'.

That was my last full summer at the St. Michael's Home for Boys in Rayburn, Georgia. My residence at the orphanage was courtesy of the 'Pedro Pan' operation. The 'Pedro Pan' or 'Peter Pan' initiative was a clandestine US instigated mass exodus of over 14,000 unaccompanied Cuban minors ages 6 to 18 to the United States over a two-year span from 1960 to 1962. Our parents go into alarm mode by unfounded rumours circulating amongst Cuban families that the new Castro government was planning to end parental rights and place minors in communist indoctrination centres in the USSR.

In February1962 a dozen young Cuban boys are placed under the care of the nuns that ran the orphanage and that was my home until the summer of 1964, but the photograph I found depicted a scene of the seven 'charioteers' in the summer of 1963.

Summer is a time when adolescent boys of all ages need to be busy or their minds will wonder into areas that while at the time seemed like a splendid idea in hindsight, the ideas can only be described as disastrous and dangerous. Our minds were idle, thus perilous thoughts are conceived and acted upon.

Back in 1959, the movie 'Ben Hur' became a blockbuster of a movie. Ben Hur was the story of a fictional hero named Judah Ben Hur, a Jewish nobleman who is falsely accused and convicted of an attempted assassination of the Roman governor of Judaea and consequently enslaved by the Romans. The nine-minute chariot race has become one of cinema's most famous action sequences, and the score, composed and conducted by Miklós Rózsa, is the longest ever composed of a film. But it was the chariot race that inspired us to recreate it, using our bicycles as chariots.

In order to 'spice up' the action, we would get as many old Gillette double edge shaving blades as we could, and we attached them to the spokes of the bicycles with the sole purpose of inflicting punctures in the bicycle tyres and disabling our opponent's chariots during the race. It was awesome to see the double edge blades glimmer in the midday sun.

The course was a simple course shaped somewhat circularly as best as we could do in the area in which we could ride the bicycles away from the prying eyes of the nuns. To make the race interesting, we threw in a few obstacles in the middle of the racecourse (old wheelbarrows, chairs) anything that would make life more interesting, or so we thought.

We got eight bicycles all setup with all of them having at least six double edge blades in both the front and rear tyres and so eight young charioteers took their position while the other four monitored the race and kept a lookout for the nuns. The other four boys (Pedro, Juan, Carlos, and Miguel) had their own responsibilities with lap counter (Pedro), obstacle course manager (Juan), photographer (Carlos) and lookout, Miguel.

The race started, and mostly it was exciting and boring at the same time. The excitement was the many attempts at trying to puncture the tyres of the opponent's bicycles while the boredom was seeing no success by anyone of the charioteers.

The race is to be for ten laps (the movie had nine) but we thought that ten would be a better number and besides, we have ten fingers, so it is easier to count the laps. So, for first seven laps nothing happens, but at the beginning of lap number eight, Alberto takes a quick swerve at Mateo's rear tyre and misses. Instead of puncturing the rear tyre, Alberto got Mateo's left leg and a chuck of his calf comes off with a waterfall of blood streaming down Mateo's leg.

Suddenly there was a panic after Mateo gave off the most awful sounding scream of pain after he felt the cut and the screaming became louder when Mateo looked down at his left leg all bloodied.

Miguel was on the further post and saw what had happened and started running towards the home to get the chief nun, Sister Francis, for help.

Sister Francis, Sister Magdalene, and Sister Alberta are running like wild penguins towards us and reaching Mateo, they place a quick compression on his leg and the nuns carried him off to the home's infirmary for mending.

The boys stood in the makeshift racecourse watching the nuns take the wounded charioteer Mateo to the infirmary.

No one was in shock, but we wondered what the nuns would do to us next.

It did not matter for the race had happened and then Francisco said, 'Let us find Mateo's piece of leg as a trophy.' It seemed like a grand idea and as we searched the dusty makeshift racecourse, we find the piece of Mateo's

91

calf all bloodied, covered in dirt and we held it up high as Miguel takes the photograph of the 1963 chariot race at the St. Michael's Home for Boys.

Those were happy times!

THE TRAIN JOURNEY

A round this time of the year, I get that mushy feeling. A feeling that lets me know that summer has passed. Autumn is around the corner, and I am ready for it. I see the leaves falling from the trees, like early snowflakes at Thredbo. My wife and I start our train journey during this time of the year. We love it and this year is no different and again; we hit the tracks with no point in mind. The reason; is the sound.

There is nothing like the sound of a train as it leaves a station. The steadily increasing chugging sound as the train picks up speed. Then you hear the train running on its rails. The constant repetitive clickety-clackety sound you hear from the plates that join the rails; when your train passes over them, you hear those sounds.

Clickety-clackety.

Clickety-clackety.

Clickety-clackety.

The sound just can put you to sleep if you are not careful.

As the train travels faster toward its destination, the sounds become more of a rumbling sound journeying through valleys and fields all the while. Its whistle sounds like a lonely call in the night. The brakes shush and screech when the train slows down to a crawl as it arrives at its destination.

Other sounds will appear during our train journey, but they seem to be drowned out by the rhapsody of the train as it lulls us, calling us to repeat the journey, year after year.

Who needs the noise of an airplane as it shears through the air-masses?

Who needs the ear-splitting noise of a bus travelling down a highway?

We sit back and wait for when we both fall asleep as we listen to the most soothing sound of a train.

Clickety-clackety.

Clickety-clackety.

Clickety-clackety.

Clickety-clackety.

Clickety-clackety.

Clickety-clackety

THE WHITE BEARDED ONE

The day arrived and there was nothing I could do about it. I had postponed, delayed, staled, and reschedule the day but I no longer had any more excuses it had to get done. I am horrified. The abscess tooth had to be taken care of.

I parked at the Westfield's Penrith mall since there was no reasonable long-term parking at the endodontist office. I rapidly marched the twelve-minute walk towards the inevitable session with 'el barburo blanco'.

The translation of 'el barbudo blanco' is 'the white bearded one' but to me I thought of him more like the infamous Nazi war criminal Dr. Christian Szell from the movie 'Marathon Man'.

Arriving at the office, I am immediately ushered into the chair where the procedure (could I say torture) will take place. The white bearded one smiles as he approaches my face and simply says; 'Let's begin'.

Two quick shots of novocaine appear to do the trick with my jaw feeling numb and without asking, the white bearded one starts. Just like in the movie scene that shows Szell torturing Babe (Dustin Hoffman) with dental instruments and the actual on-screen drilling of Babe's tooth, I could feel the pain through every nerve in my body.

Suddenly I hear; 'Wake up. You are all done.'

I open my eyes and realise that I had been dreaming the scene from the movie and that I actually had no pain from the procedure. The white bearded one was excellent at his work.

As I leave, the receptionist calls out my name and hands me the bill for the procedure. I glance at it and realise that the horror is just beginning...........

THERE IS ALWAYS NEXT YEAR

It has always amazed me how commercial a lot of the holidays have become. Christmas, Easter seems to have lost all their meanings and the tinsels of the festivities, Santa Claus, the Easter Bunny, are flourishing. There is, however, one holiday period that was designed for making money, Valentine's Day.

We assume the story of Valentine Day to go all the way back to the time of Emperor Claudius II Gothicus. They nicknamed him Claudius the Cruel because of his harsh leadership. He was a darn bad emperor since he was running short of men to fight his wars, he prohibited Roman soldiers from marrying or getting engaged since a lot of the soldiers just did not want to leave their wives and family to fight in Claudius II wars.

Enter a priest by the name of Valentine, who married in secret the soldiers before they went off to war. When Claudius found out, he threw Valentine into jail and ordered him to be executed.

On the eve of his execution, with nothing to write with legend says that Valentine wrote a sonnet in ink that he squeezed from violets to the daughter of his jailer. The legend then states that his words made the blind woman see again. This is a delightful story that ended with poor Valentine being clubbed to death by Roman executioners the next day.

That is the legend. Now let me share with you what really happened.

The first Valentine's Day was in the year 496, and it was started by one of my ancestors in ancient Rome, I can provide written proof, Thaddeus Faustus created the first romantic granite note to his lover, Florentina Valentina, and having seen the results of the note trademarked the name 'Valentina's Day' and since that time, the money has been pouring into the family coffers. Not sure when the confusion with the priest Valentine started, but the tradition of Valentina's Day began when Thaddeus sent Valentina that first granite note. The legend you hear is fake news. '

Wars, famines, pestilence, nothing has stopped the spread of Valentina's Day and the money just keeps coming in. The granite notes gave way to letters, along came the first cards in 1415. Then came the telegrams, then email, and, of course, Facebook. Zuckerberg is a distant cousin in case you did not know, but Valentine Day cards are irreplaceable and will continue making money for my family.

So, I wanted to thank you for spending your retirement money or salary money, or savings money on a nice card for your partner this February 14th, 2020. My family thanks you from the bottom of our bank's vaults.

If you forgot, then remember, there is always next year!

95

WAS THAT REALLY THE EASTER BUNNY?

The late 1960s' were full of exciting things happening, some good and some not so good. My wife was always harping me about picking up hitchhikers when we were out for a drive. Picking up hitchhikers was such a common thing that if there was one day when you did not see a hitchhiker, well, that meant you did not go out that day. Picking up hitchhikers is something I did then and still do in this much stranger times.

So here we were driving down Carrols Road on the way to our home in Menangle New South Wales when right smack in front of us in the middle of the road stands a 2-metre-tall rabbit holding a basket and has his thumb sticking out hoping for a ride.

I look at my wife and say: 'Hey, let us give this guy a ride. I bet he is on the way to an Easter party somewhere.' My wife sounds off the alarm: 'Never You Be Trusting A Stranger' but I remember reading in the old King James Bible version a saying that suggested that if you see a person in need on the side of the road, you help them so I stop.

Slowing down to a complete halt, I roll the glass of my driver's window and take a better look at the dressed-up bunny. I am impressed. The costume was of superior quality. Must have been Aussie made for sure, I thought. A nice furry feel to the topcoat I sensed as the bunny stands next to the window and poises his arm on the open window.

'Mate, what a relief that you stopped. You must have been the third car to go by in five hours and not a one stopped. Thanks a lot, mate!' says the big bunny with a funny accent.

Offering an enormous smile, I ask: 'Where are you heading?'

'I am hoping to reach the Franklin farm over in Jenkins Street way. You would not be going that way, perchance?' asks the big bunny.

'I know where that is, but I believe Joe Franklin sold the spread a while back and no one has taken residence yet. Are you sure that is the direction you want to head to?' I ask.

'Oh yes. I received an email saying that we should all congregate there this week to discuss our plans for Easter.' The bunny answered in a serious tone.

My wife nudges me showing she thought sometime suspicious, or nutty, was going on with this guy and that we should drive away.

Eyeing the big bunny and taking heed of my wife's nudge, I ask: 'You ain't some spaced out, stoned, hippie just hoping for a good smoke out over the empty Franklin estate, is ya?' I demanded.

'No sir, you would make an inaccurate perception of me.' The big bunny answered.

I was happy with the answer. I nodded to my wife to keep hushed up and said. 'Then hop in, the Franklin farm ain't far and I do not mind dropping you off.' As the big bunny gets in the back seat, he sets himself in, but he must first fold his big bunny ears down to fit.

Trying to be friendly, I ask: 'Where ya come from?'

The big bunny was happy to answer because he went into telling the story in which he said his family were of old German stock which had first immigrated to and settled in Pennsylvania USA in the 1700s but as time passed all the descendants themselves emigrated to other parts of the world.

So, I ask, 'What brings you all the way out here?'

'My colony is gathering together to discuss the current COVID-19 crisis and how we will handle it this Easter season and we have taken to meet at the Franklin farm to discuss ideas.' the bunny answers nonchalant like.

My mind tries to make sense of the story and answers given by the big bunny, and I realise; this guy is one huge lunatic!

Just then, I turned my Holden Cruze into the old Franklin farm so my wife and I would not have to listen to these strange stories or have the strange company of the big bunny for much longer.

As I pull up to where the old house should have been standing, there is nothing there, just the largest yellow basket you have ever seen. It was easily forty metres wide and twenty metres high with a massive red door.

'Thank you for your help. I shall not be late for our conference. You have been of great service to me,' the big bunny said.

Getting out of the car, the bunny reaches into his own basket to reveal a huge golden egg, shimmering and decorated with beautiful lines.

'As a token of my appreciation please accept this golden egg which will make all of your future Easter gatherings very festive,' says the big bunny as he handed me the egg and heads towards the huge basket, opens the red door, turns, and waves and disappears into the basket.

Starting the car, I hand the golden egg to my wife and as we hit the road again, I ask my wife; 'Do you think that was really the Easter bunny?'

YOU CAN'T NAME YOUR BABY THAT!

Summer has arrived in Sydney and it is December 12 and it is time to introduce our new baby to all our family and friends.

It has been one hell of a ride with tensions around the world; the market is going up and down, but mostly down. The insecurity of either of us would have a job and the Australian government, in its infinitesimal wisdom, giving the public contradictory recommendations of how to live our lives.

Does not matter, we survived and now we are gathering here today to share, on this most momentous day, the naming of our child.

We have taken our time and review all our possibilities. Our ancestral surnames from both sides of the family are strong, virile, and soothing, so we must find a first name to complement our combined surnames.

The library provided several books on names such as *Baby Names Australia–2020*, *The Best Baby Names for Boys*, *The Best Baby Names for Girls* (we did not know what the sex was until the day of birth) so we needed to be prepared. We also borrow *The Best Baby Names for Jewish Children* and *The Best Baby Names for Christian Children* On a lark, we also checked out *The Modern Book of Muslim Names* since the Bible already has a lot of old names in it and maybe we could get an idea.

We spent hours reviewing each book and selecting the best from each book, or at least we thought they were the best for our child, yet to be born. Add to this pressure, the family suggestions came from both sides of the family. 'Your great uncle's name was Bartholomew. Your great aunt was Agatha, you know, like in Christie', and so forth and so on. Our family bombarded us until we put our foot down and told everyone on both sides of the family to stop that we had this.

After a day of reprieve from the families, the suggestions started coming from well-meaning friends. You were born in the 60s, name the baby a cool hippie name. Like Dude, Flower or Elixir! Finally, our friends also received the stern warning that we had it under control.

So, the day has arrived and our families and closest of friends gathered around our lounge room waiting in anticipation. My wife takes the floor and starts the announcement.

'My dearest family and friends, both Jengo and I are so happy that you have taken time to come here today and share in this auspicious occasion. The naming of our first child.'

A lot of hoorays. Loud whistling start and I quickly hush them since we do not want to wake the baby and I nod to my wife to continue.

'As I mentioned, Jengo and I have spent an enormous amount of time researching what we hope is the best name for our child. We welcomed all of your suggestions, but this is very personal for me and Jengo so we insist on coming up with the name ourselves and we did. The name was right there in front of us all the time, but we did not see it until one night. I want Jengo to tell you the rest of this story, Jengo,' please continue.

I stand and continue the prepared speech: 'Thank you, Betlinde. Our marriage has been a blessing for us both. Betlinde comes from a strong German background while I come from a proud Swahili background. Choosing a first name that can carry both the strength and the pride of both our cultures is especially important to us. To both our families. We feel we have done so with our chosen name to go with our hyphenated last name– Neun-Kijana. So, we are proud today to announce the name, here, to our family and friends.'

I nod to Betlinde to gather the child in the nursery. A few moments pass and the room is in anticipation and out comes Betlinde with the most beautiful caramel colour skin child you have ever seen since the beginning of time.

The men clap softly, and the women begin 'ohs and ahs' in a low tone as to not wake the child.

Betlinde smiles and hands me the child. The child is asleep, so peaceful in this crazy world of ours. Betlinde and I are happy to have chosen the first name ourselves.

'My dear family and friends,' I begin. 'We would like to present our child to you today. Taking Betlinde's last name 'Neun' which in English translates to 'Nine' and my last name 'Kijana' which in English translates to 'Teen', we present you; Covid Neun-Kijana.

You could hear a pin drop before the entire room exploded.

I think Betlinde and I did not think this naming all the way through.

YOUR OWN CHOICE

As I journey through my life, I guess I learned a thing or two. Not really deep things, only plain old simple things that if I ever have a son, I could share with him, thus passing on some wisdom, I think.

First, there are too many women and not enough beer.

You know how you hear of so many poets, but then when you listen to them; they do not seem to bring enough rhyme to the writing. I go to a pub and have a pint and then realise that there is never enough time to enjoy it before you must leave because you have to get to work tomorrow morning.

You then realise that your own father was quite an awful sod himself, but your dog was your best friend, always.

How could I not remember that I never learned to swim, so every time I went to the river or the ocean, I just stood on the shoreline as life passes me by. Too afraid to wander in, thinking I might drown.

Grew up in the church but never got religion.

Will I rest in peace?

I guess life is what you make of it.

It is my choice. I made it.

Have you made your own choice?

A BRIEF ENCOUNTER

The moment I set eyes on him; I knew I had seen him before. I was dancing with my girlfriend in Underground Atlanta most famous dance hall–Dante's Down the Hatch. Gyrating to the best music of the era: *Dancing Queen, Staying Alive, Don't Stop till You Get Enough, December 1963, Old time Rock-and-roll* and many more. The night was blasting away and then I saw him come in.

His face was immediately recognisable and yet not one person moved toward him or even spoke to him as he came in with two gorgeous women draped in his arms and sauntered up to the dance floor.

The guy twirls both women and starts dancing what I had to say was the most awful dance moves I ever seen. Here he was a man whose face they have plastered on movie posters on the big cinema screens and he moved on the dance floor like a duck.

Like a duck, that is correct. He just waddled left and right and the two women just whirled around him sometimes, thank goodness, obscuring his dreadful dance moves.

The man starts now spinning he now is so close to me he bumps into me and almost knocks me down. He looks up at me and simply says; 'Sorry, man. Be cool!'

As he continues his embarrassing disco dance, I realise that Peter Reynolds is a lot shorter in person in that he looks on the big screen and that I seem like a giant in comparison.

This brief encounter did not mean a thing to him, but to me it made to realise that the movies are truly for entertaining and not for idolising, as many people do.

One brief encounter did this. I wonder if I had a conversation with the man what would I learn.

A GRAND ADVENTURE AWAITS

G rowing in La Habana, Cuba, was a wonderful time for me as a young lad of eleven. My parents had a beach house in the Miramar suburb, and the Caribbean Sea was a stone's throw away. When I was not attending school at the Belen Academy where I studied many wonderful subjects, one which I loved a lot, English. The reason I loved this study was because my next-door neighbour was from the USA and I believe I had a crush on Meredith, so I had an incentive. Many days when there was no school, we would venture onto the clean white sands, flopped ourselves down and just sat watching the waves roll in and as we looked into the horizon, we could see the contour of the Earth and would laugh at those early civilisations that thought the Earth was flat and if we sailed far enough, we would fall off the face of the Earth.

Sitting there, I envisioned myself always living in this beautiful part of Cuba. 'It is paradise' I would say to myself. This paradise came to a full stop in January 1959 when the Cuban Revolution disrupted the lives of many of my compatriots and Meredith left to return to the USA. A year later, my parents decided I needed to leave my current life and go live with a distant uncle and his wife in a small town called Waggalillibon in Australia.

'Australia', I said to them, 'It is at the end of the world'. Maybe I will fall off the edge of the Earth after all, I thought. I was given a letter which I was to hand to my uncle and I was told a man would meet me at the airport. He would take me to my uncle.

Arriving in Australia would be an epic journey, I thought to myself. My parents prepared me for my long journey by saying to me: 'Pepito, you will go on a grand adventure. You will travel for over 24 hours. You will leave La Habana, arrive in Mexico City, change planes, and fly to Los Angeles in the American state of California. From Los Angeles you will then do a quick a stop in the new American state of Hawaii. You will change planes again and then you will fly to Australia, landing in the early hours. You will wait a few hours and you will take another plane and fly over seven hours and arrive in a city called Perth. There a man called Lance, who speaks a little Spanish, will drive you to your uncle. When you get there. Please call us.' The last instructions my mother gave me were full of tearful eyes. She said, 'Pepito, write to us every week and do not worry, for we have planned for the airline flight attendant to take care of you during this long journey. We will see you soon.'

As I boarded the plane out of Cuba, I was scared and did everything in my power not to cry when I turned around on the tarmac and I waved at my parents even though I could not see them.

The next hours were a mixture of nervousness and excitement. The airline flight attendants all took care of me like my Mama had promised. I never was hungry or thirsty and even brought me a pillow and a blanket.

Like my Mama said, I went from plane to plane. From city to city until I landed in Perth.

Perth. Such a hard word to say. In Spanish, we do not have the 'th' sound, so every time I said it sounded like 'Perfff'. Oh well, I thought, I will not have to say too much.

As we were approaching the airport in 'Perfff' I wondered if the man that was supposed to be there to meet me might have forgotten about me, so my anxiousness built up. In my mind, I knew I was going to be OK.

An airline employee got me my bag and pointed to a man standing with a large sign with the name 'Pepito' printed on it. When I approached the man, he gave a big smile, stuck out his hand for me to shake and in the funniest accent said: 'Welcome to Australia, little mate. My name is Lance I am here to take you to your uncle'.

Lance then took me to a hilarious vehicle he called a 'Ute'. What a funny word, I thought to myself and we took off to my uncles' station. I asked Lance why did my uncle live in a station. Did he run a train? Lance threw his head back and laughed like a pirate; 'No, little mate. We call stations here what the Americans call a ranch.' Ah, so a station was a ranch, or 'rancho' as we called them in Cuba.

As we rode down the road, Lance said we had a short drive. About six hours, he said, and not to worry, for he had plenty of water and something he called 'damper'. So many funny words in Australia. I did not ask Lance what damper was because he would not stop talking. He was pointing out things to me and using many more funny names, and then he braked the 'Ute' and I almost hit my head on the dashboard.

Right in front of me was a very animal that Lance said was a wombat. 'A wombat is a cross between a bear, a pig and a gopher,' Lance said. 'It is a noble creature.'

After the wombat finished crossing the road, we started again toward Waggalillibon and as I sat there looking out the window, I could not help but think what a grand adventure awaits me.

A SENSE OF GUILT

My wife's birthday was coming up, and I failed her. It was entirely my fault. For weeks I heard my wife's hints and nothing sank into my little brain. Her hints were obvious with fine detailed words pointing me to the object of her quest.

'Camden. Diamond. Ring. Jewellery store.'

I know I heard the words. I know they were, but I thought these hints were just, well, just a hint, for my wife is a simple woman. She does not need these extravagant things.

'Aha,' the words resonated in my mind.

'Camden. Diamond. Ring. Jewellery store,'

That was not my wife speaking, I said to myself.

It has to be someone else.

Some selfish woman who took over her body and mind and this woman wanted this 'thing' and blurted out these hints.

I was not to be fooled by this woman.

The day arrived. The day of the celebration of my wife's birth. I get dressed and come downstairs and see her sitting on the breakfast counter in the kitchen. I gently give her a kiss on the top of her head and go over to the closed pantry door.

Opening the door, I reach in and pull out a brand new, spanking bright white ironing board. I turn and face my wife and with my biggest smile I say: 'Happy Birthday darling!'

Then the fight started.........

BIRTHDAY PRESENT

'Would you like to go to the cemetery?' Mum asked me and knowing she always is eager to go, I just nodded my head. It is April 1st, 2010, my birthday, and I am visiting her in Luffing Waters, my hometown of a little over 3,000 people in rural New South Wales. Sadly, I do not go back there much with my last visit back in 2001when Dad was put to rest.

My Dad was a tough bastard and never liked me.

Many a day I would receive spanking for no reason and my mum never intervened or said anything to him. My Mum and I never really spoke about my dad and our strange relationship. Many nights I laid in my bed crying myself to sleep and my mum never came in to console me, so she was also never high on my list, but I accepted all this and as soon as I could, I left Luffing Waters for Sydney.

'You know, Billy, I do not get to see you much these days'. Mum softly says to me while in the car.

'I know Mum. With work, the kids and since the death or Mary, my weekends are doing stuff and fix things around the house and get ready to spend the weekend with the kids. I should make more of an effort. I am sorry.' I am hoping this kind of apology would ease my lack of visitation with Mum and she not seeing her grandchildren as often.

We stay quiet for longer, but I decide to ask Mum some questions to have at least a pleasant conversation she might remember me for.

'Mum, when you come to the cemetery, what do you do?'

'Mostly, I make sure the flowers are still inside the vase because sometimes the wind just blows them away. I also replace the ones that might have been worn out by the sun. Mostly I make sure your Dad's name, Angus, still can be read, and it is nice and clean so I can see it as I approach the tombstone. Finally, I also make sure that my tombstone next to his is also nice and clean and ready for when it is my time.'

'I know you do, Mum. You have always been grand about that.' I say, putting a smile on her old face.

As we gently turn into and go down the road that leads us to the Emerald Hills Memorial Gardens Mum mumbles out loud to herself and making comments how nice the cemetery looks and how well maintained it is and what a magnificent place will be to rest for eternity. Again, I see a beautiful smile on the old face.

'Here Billy. Turn here. See the tombstones on that side over there with all the Australian flags.' my mother instructs, pointing to her left. When I utter

Oh, yes, she continues, 'Billy, you have not been here in such a long time you forgotten where my dear Angus, your Father, lies in his peaceful rest.'

Though I know the answer, I answer, 'Yes I know Mum' as much to make an agreement with her and not repeat my reasons for not visiting.

Arriving at the exact location Mum pointed out to me, I stop the car and help her out and as we wander into the cemetery and to my parent's tombstones, I discovered an adjacent tombstone engraved with my name and date of birth — the date of death had been left blank!

My eyes almost popped out of my eye socket when I saw this and all I could think was, this some kind of prank?

I turn to my Mother who, with a big smile, says in a loud voice; 'Now Billy, is this not a pleasant surprise for your birthday?'

Staring at my very own tombstone, I ask; 'Mum, what makes you think that this is an appropriate birthday present to give your only son? What makes you think I would be buried here? Did you ever think I might want to be buried next to Mary? What if I remarry? Would I not want to be buried with my new wife or she with me if I go first?'

Mum takes a moment or two in deep thought and then she comes out with a surprising answer. 'Billy, have you never noticed that I never liked Mary? God bless her soul! I always thought that she was not right for you. She was always spending your hard-earned money on frivolous things and over decorating the house and going on awfully expensive holidays. I never understood why she had to holiday in Sydney. What is wrong with Bathurst, really?'

Knowing I would regret anything I might say and Mum would be mad at me forever I had nothing to lose, so I simply turned and left her there, by Dad's, grave and if she did not like it, well, she could join him.

Placing the key in the car started, I sense, again, a loneliness that I felt in my youth, but this time it is not making me cry but a feeling that I was finally free from my demons.

JOIN THE TEAM

'No. No way we should hire him,' said Abigail. 'This will be his first job! Think about it! His very first job! He brings no experience, he brings no knowledge, nothing.'

Taking it all in, I mull my answer and then I ask. 'Why not Abigail? Why not give him a chance? Look at his photo. He is perfect for the type of missions we go on.'

'Wait just a moment,' jumping in Gayle. 'He looks great in the photograph, but can he handle the stress of the job? Is his mental fortitude strong enough to withstand the pressures of the assignments we go on? I am not sure?'

'Well, I think he can,' chimes in Beatrice. 'Look at his CV! It is a pure delight to read. He brings degrees in biochemistry and molecular biology, mathematical science, psychology, and to top the list, he speaks the top six languages in the world: Chinese Mandarin, Spanish, Hindi, Bengali, Portuguese, Russian, and his native tongue, English. That makes up 36% of the world's population.'

'Still, I am not convinced. I hear your comments, all valid, as I mentioned, I am not convinced,' prompts in Abigail.

'OK, how about his physical skills?' I add.

Abigail looks at his CV and shares her thoughts.

'Right. He possesses some valuable martial arts skills. Let's see. He has high levels of status in Karate, Kung Fu, Muay Thai, Brazilian Jiu-Jitsu and Krav Maga. Quite impressive, but really is that enough?'

Heads are nodding in every direction from the team. The team is divided with a few nodding yes while others nodding no but suddenly, like a chain reaction, there is unison in the nods, all in the affirmative but one: Abigail.

That is, it. I need to conclude this meeting. Looking straight at her, I thrust the question on Abigail.

'What is it about him you just cannot accept. What reason can he not join our team, Abigail?'

Abigail takes her best shot and, looking at the entire team and with a serious face, responds to my question.

'He looks better in a dress that all of us.'

Our laughter went viral and after we calmed down, we decide that any man that can look better than any of us in a dress is worthy to join the team.

I SEE NOTHING BUT RED

The moment I opened my father's front door, a sense of sadness just overtook me, for my mission today was to go through the house and sort out his belongings since his passing.

It had been well over three years since I visited and I noticed a lot of changes as soon as I open his red front door.

Dad had obviously done some remodelling in the past few years and he had ventured into some extremes, which was nothing like him.

Starting with the red door to the red shutters, which made for an interesting and rather striking facade to the red velvety curtains in both the lounge and in all three bedrooms.

Even the furniture took its own fiery red colour with both the lounge, the recliner, and the side chair in vibrant red colours.

What took me aback was his library collection of books. Placed in white IKEA bookcases, thank goodness he did not paint the bookcases red, was a collection of over 1000-books and the unique thing about them were the titles.

Starting with the *'Hunt for Red October'* to *'Red Storm Rising'* and *'Red Rabbit'*, these two last ones were a part of a large accumulation of Tom Clancy's published works. I glanced at the collection and wanders if Dad had actually read them all.

He had a first edition of Edgar Allan Poe's *'The Masque of the Red Death'* published in 1805 which had to be worth a fortune and John Steinbeck's first edition published in 1933 of *'The Red Pony'* and to my delight Stephen Crane's *'The Red Badge of Courage'* first edition published in 1895. Again, another treasure, and most likely quite valuable as well.

In this collection, Dad even had children's books, which I know for a fact he never shared with any of his grandchildren. Titles such as *'Clifford the Big Red Dog'*, *'One Fish Two Fish Red Fish Blue Fish'*, *'Little Red Riding Hood'*, *'The Adventures of Chatterer the Red Squirrel'* and even *'Amber Brown Sees Red'*.

His taste in books I thought made him quite a bibliophile for even his assortment of books contained travel books (*'The Big Red Train Ride,'*) and historical books (*'Red Victory: A History of the Russian Revolution,'* and *'Red Horizons: The True Story of Nicolae and Elena Ceausescu's Crimes, Lifestyle and Corruption,'*) as well as *'Red Storm Over the Balkans: The Failed Soviet Invasion of Romania, Spring 1944,'* to name just a few.

To my surprise, Dad even had books on sports, which is quite a surprise since he never even kicked a soccer ball with me. However, his variety of books on this subject included 'Red Smith on Baseball', also 'Detroit Red Wings Greatest Moments and Players' and 'How the Boston Red Sox Won the World Series'.

Another big surprise was a few books in erotica. With titles like 'Red Hot Erotica' and a few others with I care not to mention.

After my perusal of the library, I ventured to Father's bedroom. Oh boy. Walking into the room, I found more red. A lot more red. Red filled the room. From a red bedspread, red window trimmings, and a red accent wall, my dad had gone from strange to weird, I thought, until I reach the ensuite.

Wonderful. At least the toilet is red!

Carefully opening the ensuite door, I find a blaze of red. Red toilet seat, red bidet, red bathtub, and the shower screen was a light burgundy, all coordinated with the white and red towels strategically placed on red and white cabinets in the ensuite.

As I began sorting through his closet and chest drawers, again a cascade of red popped out to me. Red shirts, red pants, a couple of red and white golf shoes and again, a red and white flapper pair of shoes like those used in the 1920s. I am embarrassed to say even red underwear.

It took me a couple of weeks to document, sort and catalogue the contents of my Dad's home and I came up with the conclusion that the reason my dad loved the colour red was because red is reported to make individuals more attractive. Seeing others in front of red backgrounds, you find those other individuals as more attractive than when they see them silhouetted against other colours, thus my Dad used red for the bedroom wall. Using red also gives us a burst of strength, so reds are wonderful choices for someone who might need that extra confidence.

As I left my Dad's home, I promised myself that I would not judge him but embrace some, not all, of his quirks since red is also a wonderful wine colour and I love wine.

IN THE COFFEE SHOP

In the coffee shop, she waited for the individual that left her the strange note under her dorm room door.

'Meet me at the coffee shop at 10 AM today. I have important information for you. Bring a pad and pen.' They signed it with an E.

Waiting and waiting was not a quality that Liz possessed, but she was getting out of her stenography class for this peculiar meeting, and it intrigued her. She was being tested because as she glances at the clock on the wall, the clock struck 10 AM and then she heard the little bell that is attached to the front door of the coffee shop.

In walks a handsome young man, and he heads straight to her. In anticipation, she straightens up, hoping this is her anonymous new fan and smiles and he just walks past and he heads straight to the counter where she hears him say; 'Black coffee, please. No sugar.'

Looking at him, she wonders if that is him just getting a coffee before sitting next to her when she feels her shoulder being tapped. Startled, she turns and finds an older mature looking woman, probably in her late fifties or early sixties, who smiles and says: 'He is not in your destiny, dear. Now listen carefully and write everything I tell you. Be quick, girl, for I have little time.'

'Who are you?', she asks.

Without answering her question, the older woman babbles strange words and points to the notepad and does the air sign for writing in the air and she, without hesitation, has no choice but to write what the older woman says.

Ordinary words and strange words, one after the other. Some are recognisable as apple, but other she never heard of. Words as bitcoin, Canva, Zoom, Moderna, Amazon, Costco, Netflix, Nvidia, Nio and Uber.

She continues writing more words; Alibaba, Sony, Tupperware, and many more that after a minute the paper is full of words with no meaning to her.

Then the older woman stops speaking, smiles and turns towards the front to door to exit.

'Wait', as she runs behind her but realises, she left her pen and pad on the table and goes and retrieves her them. As she goes out the door, she looks left and then right and sees her. There is the old crazy woman, she thinks, turning into the alley. I must catch up with her. I must know what I am supposed to do with all this gibberish.

Running toward the alley, she turns and suddenly stops and sees a huge circular light in a spinning fast motion. The light is covering the entire end of the alley and the older woman is standing there waiting. Waiting for what, she wonders.

Sensing her, the older woman turns. Again, she smiles and says, 'For once in your life, Liz, follow instructions and look out for those words. They will be better than any of those crazy men you have been dreaming about.' Then the older woman turns and walks into the light and disappears in a flash.

Stunned, Liz stands there wondering who this Elizabeth is, and what she wants her to do with these words, but something in her mind tells her that in the coffee shop just a few minutes ago she had just seen herself in the future.

LISTEN TO YOUR HEART

'Mum! Why did you pull me off, Michael? I had him down for the first time. Ever! The very first time!' I exploded at my mother.

Michael Howell is my neighbourhoods' bully. He has been constantly bullying me and my friends simply because he can. For a ten-year-old boy, he is huge, no massive would be a better description. Weighting seventy kilos and one hundred and one hundred sixty-five centimetres tall, he is like a mountain in my grade five with Miss McDonald. I stand at 144 centimetres and 61 kilos by comparison, so when stands in front of me at assembly, the teachers cannot see me.

'I told you, Billy, to avoid Michael Howell at all times, and yet here you were in a fight with him. I am so glad I saw it and pull you out before he hurt you.'

'Mum, you pull me out at the wrong time. I had him down. I was ready to punch him in the face. Finally, I could get back on him and his bullying and the moment I make that happen, the first time, you grab my arm and yank me off of him. Why?'

'Again, I am not repeating myself. You should not be fighting. That is why I pull you off him. Now tell me what provoked this fight?'

'Mum, you know today is June 21st, 2021, Monday, right?'

'Of course, Billy, I know. What of it?'

'Did you know today is the shortest day of the year?'

'No, I did not. What does that have to do with you and Michael Howell getting into a fistfight?'

'Well Mum, Michael said that since today is the shortest day of the year that I should wear the shortest skirt my sister has in her closet since I am shorter than she is'.

'So, this little tease started the fight?'

'Yes, Mum it was.'

'Billy, why did you just not walk away?'

'I took your advice this time, Mum. I did what you suggested.'

'What? I never said for you to fight, Michael. When did I say such a thing?'

'When you told me last time when I got into a fight with him to listen to my heart. So, I did.'

PARALYSED WITH FEAR

Paralysed with fear, Jessica struggled to decide on her next course of action. The moment had arrived for a quick decision and there she stood, unable to decide as to her next move. This is the first time Jessica had frozen and could not make a decisive choice in a long time. Every day, three times a day, twenty-one times a week, one-thousand and ninety-five times a year, she had pondered what to do and arrive at a conclusive answer, but not at this moment.

What happen?

Have her creative juices stopped flowing?

Have her creative juices been drained after all these many years and she is left now empty?

Has her planning muse stopped working for her?

Jessica felt a lapse of concentration and attention - she felt confabulated a little, she said to herself.

To help, Jessica proposed to herself she open a bottle of Penfolds Bin 169 Cabernet Sauvignon 2016 and at $359.00 a bottle, she mumbled– 'This better help'.

Downing one glass after another and savouring the primarily blackcurrant, crème de cassis, black olive, aniseed, with a hint of violet flavour, Jessica fells she has wasted a wonderful drop since not one new thought of creativity comes into her mind.

The Penfolds failed her, but Jessica had an arsenal available to her, so she opened a second bottle of wine. This time a French selection–a Chateau des Deux Rives Bordeaux 2016 costing $240.00 and hopes that its pleasant red berry aromas, with its hint of fresh walnut and toasted vanilla and its fresh, well-rounded fruit driven mixture, will inspire her today.

Feeling a bit wobbly, Jessica still does not know what to do when her teenage son walks in and says: 'Mum, what are we having for dinner?'

Jessica continues to stand there paralyse in fear for she still has no answer.

ST. PATRICKS' DAY

There are many stories about how St. Patrick Day was established and today the reader will read the one authentic version, and I believe the reader will be surprised.

On a beautiful Sunday morning Patricio was walking the warm, sandy beaches of El Miramar in La Habana Cuba when he noticed a large ship offshore and he saw a rowboat full of Caribbean pirates lowered from its side and once on the water the rowboat started rowing toward the shore straight at him.

This sight just captivated Patricio as he stood on the shoreline and with the waves just lapping at his feet, he stood there mesmerised. He felt excited for he, at eleven years of age, had heard many stories about the Caribbean pirates but never had seen one, and there were now three of them on the rowboat coming towards him.

Upon landing on the shore in a split second, the pirates grab Patricio, throwing him to the bottom of the rowboat and quickly returning to their ship, which set sail to new worlds unknown to Patricio.

After weeks on the open ocean, Patricio sees land for the first time and sees the luscious landscape spreading itself in front of him and a large port city which he heard the pirate called 'Portus'. After landing on terra firma after so many weeks, they rushed Patricio into a large warehouse and they sold him as a slave to work on the fields.

Patricio worked ridiculously hard in the fields for his master and pray for someone to liberate him and then one day Patricio hears a voice telling him to escape which he did and walked all the way back to the port city of Portus and he found a ship going to the port city of Cork. Having never heard of Cork Patricio decided that anything beats his current lifestyle, so he got on the ship heading to Cork.

As he sailed to Cork Patricio daydreams of his birth in Cuba and that fateful day on the beach and his capture by the Caribbean pirates. Growing up to adulthood near the port city of Portus and nor could he not forget how the voice that had saved him while in that miserable place Portus. He decided that once he reached this unknown land called 'Cork' he would get as many people as possible to listen to his story of the voice that spoke to him.

Patricio travelled far and wide throughout the land he later learned was named Ireland telling everyone his story but the Druid priests would get mad with him because he was obviously threating their domain but that did not deter Patricio for, he had many adventures, escapades, and stories to share with the people of Ireland primarily the women.

Men were taking too long to propose to women in Ireland at the time of Patricio's travels, so Patricio thought about this issue and concluded he had a solution to the problem. Patricio started telling the women that it was OK for women to ask men to marry and if a man refused the proposal, Patricio said the man should give the woman one hundred pounds or a silk dress which Patricio thought would be a fair deal. The idea took off splendidly. Many women started asking the men to marry and if they refused, well, the women would at least get something in return. There are so many stories attributed to Patricio and the many wonderful things that he did, like getting rid of the snakes in Ireland. The citizens of Ireland adopted Patricio as their own, similar to how Australians have adopted the Bee Gees and claimed them as Australian and not British. The Irish populace then changed his name from Patricio to Patrick. By the time of his death on March 17th Patricio, now more known as Patrick, had done a lot of good and later he was proclaimed a patron saint for Ireland.

So now you know the true story of how a young Cuban boy became one of the patron saints of Ireland and why we celebrate St. Patrick's Day to this date.

THE BLUE WOOLLEN COAT

The first thing I notice is the cold. It hurts my face. Never had I ever felt something like this sting. It feels like pins and needles on my face, arms, legs, all over my eleven-year-old body. Stepping off the plane onto the tarmac at Atlanta Municipal Airport that January morning was a significant moment, for I had landed in the land of opportunity, according to my parents.

Walking through the terminal, the coldness of the place continues to haunt me and would not leave me and both my parents knew this for they also felt the bitterness of the weather as we walked outside to meet my parents' friends.

Totally unprepared, I thought we were.

Khaki shorts, blue shirt with short sleeves, and flip-flops were our outfits straight out of a Caribbean beach scene. It made sense since we came from a Caribbean island to the freezing tundras of Atlanta. For what reason I asked my father on the plane?

'To escape', was his answer.

Escape?

From what I wondered? I did not know. I was told that we were going on a holiday, but no way did these events resemble any holiday I ever remember being on.

'There. There are Miguel and Luz,' my mother motions.

After what seemed a lifetime of hugs, kisses, and sobs, they direct the attention towards me and my shaking in the wind.

'The boy must be freezing. Let us get out of this wind and go get him a coat.'

Climbing into the 1962 Ford Fairlane, I huddled between my mother and father in the back seat and felt like a small bird warmed in its nest as my parents covered me. I was warming up a little as the Fairlane barrelled down the interstate towards the store to buy us all some coats.

'We are taking you to the Sears Roebuck & Co at Ponce de Leon Avenue. It is fantastic,' said Luz as she turned around from the front seat and spoke to my parents.

As we approached the building, I was in a wonderment.

Never had I seen such a huge, no, gigantic building, for it stood well over ten floors high. Parking the Fairlane, we ventured inside and immediately felt the warm air against my face. 'It has central heat. It is quite advanced and comfortable. They make it quite nice to shop in here,' explained Miguel to my parents, who were as awe struck as I was.

'They are having quite a sale of just about everything. It is the after Christmas sale so we should be able to get a few nice coats for you today,' added Luz as she herded my mother towards the coats.

Coats, coats, and more coats. They covered the entire floor in coats of all sizes, colours, and textures. Many had signs with big letters 'SALE' while others had 'REDUCED' signs, but these apparently did not attract Luz's interest. Luz bee-lined to an enormous sign in large letters 'CLEARANCE' and she took us all in that direction.

Here we found an even larger variety of coats for girls, boys, women, and men again in all styles, and colours, so many, that I thought we would be still in the store until sundown deciding on what to buy.

They did not ask for my opinion. They gave me coat after coat to try on, and my mother and Luz commented on how I settled into the coat while Miguel and my father took turns trying on coats. Miguel said he did not have a need for one but like just trying on the coats to make sure 'I have gained no weight from Luz's 'arroz con pollo' as he chuckles, helping my father with a brown coat.

Suddenly my mother gasps as she grabs a blue woollen coat from the 'CLEARANCE,' rack. 'This is just a beautiful coat. Look at the brilliant blue colour. It will go so well with Jose's complexation. I think I found the perfect coat for him,' says my mother as she glances at me in full triumph and hands me the coat to try on.

I try on the coat.

It is huge on me.

It does not sit well.

The arms are way too large for me and extend past my hands by at least six inches. The coat length is also way too huge for me. It makes me look like I have a potato sack on and not a coat.

I hate it, and yet......

As the minutes pass, I look in the floor-length mirror and see the bright blue colour radiating the sea colours from home and I felt the wool slowly caressing my skin, its warmth blending with the 'central heat' and making me feel all safe, all secure, and warm.

My father takes my left hand, looks at the tag dangling from the coat's arm, smiles and says proudly; 'We will take it'.

As we drive to Miguel and Luz's home sitting in the back of the Fairlane, I huddle again even closer between my parents in my new blue woollen coat and I know I have found a new friend in this chilly place called Atlanta.

THE COLLECTOR

The moment I opened my eyes, I know it was going to be a great day!
The feeling of success was overpowering as I went downstairs, opened the door, and I retrieved the morning paper from my front lawn. Yes, today was the day I will find my new career. Eagerly, I made a coffee and sat down at the breakfast counter and searched for the ultimate position that would lead me into a new career.

There it was, front and centre, in the second column of the classified:

'Looking for an exciting career working with individuals? Enjoy working with clients and staff? Love identifying, locating, and notifying individuals of overdue accounts in person and arranging for payments to be made? Have a passion for arranging for the collection of a debt to be transferred to creditors' possession and preparing_statements of account for the creditor. If so, visit our office at 13 Main Street, Level 13, Suite 13, Camden NSW 1313.'

This is it, I thought. This sounds like the perfect career move. I quickly finished my coffee, ran upstairs, and got dressed in the best suit I have and headed to my future profession.

Arriving at 13 Main Street, I walked into the building and onto a lift, punched level 13 and as the doors open, I see a sign pointing left to Suite 13. I eagerly go in that direction to apply for this position before anyone else.

Opening the door, a small reception area there awaited me a couple of comfortable chairs. Another door with the inscription 'Mr. Luciferous' imprinted on the smoky glass door and a small desk occupied by an older grumpy-looking lady who did not look happy to be there but said: 'Are you here for the position?'

'Yes, I am. Is there an application form I need to complete?', I asked.

Handing me a clipboard with one sheet on it and a pen, she pointed to a chair for me to sit and complete the paperwork. I have completed many job applications before and this one was by far the simplest form I have ever seen. All it asks was four questions: Full name. How long I have lived in town. Date of birth. Contact details.

Quite interesting, I thought as I completed the form. I handed it back to the lady and again she motions for me to sit. She then knocks on the door and goes in. I did as I was told and sat comfortably waiting to be called for my interview.

After a few minutes, the grumpy old lady comes out of the office and says: 'He is ready to see you. Go on in.'

Well, that was quick, I thought as I excitingly get up from the chair and am ushered into Mr. Luciferous office.

Entering the office, I find a luxurious office with oak furniture, bookcases with many files and one of the largest desks I have ever seen, with one amazingly comfortable chair fronting the desk. Behind I see Mr Luciferous wearing an expensive business suit crafted from the world's most expensive wools—vicuna and qiviut. Vicuna fleece is the symbol of ultimate luxury. They are close relatives of the llama and are native to Peru. The tiny vicuna produces incredibly warm and soft wool known as "The Silk of the New World." The total world supply is only twelve tonnes per year. No surprise then that it costs more than gold! I know this because for a few months I worked for Alexander Amosu and I learned a lot but fail as a salesperson of business suits.

Mr Luciferous is one handsome man. From the depth of his eyes to the gentle expressions on his face. As soon as he welcomes me, I loved the way his voice quickened when he asked me to sit.

'Please sit have a seat, Albert. May I call you Albert?'

As I sunk into the amazing chair, Mr Luciferous started into the interview.

'I see you live in town for twenty years. You must know a lot of individuals that live in the area?'

'Why yes I do. The beauty of a small town is you get to meet a lot of your neighbours over the years and sometimes it even becomes a generational occurrence where you meet the grandparents, then the parents and finally the children of one entire household. A pleasurable experience,' I answer.

Mr Luciferous then asks; 'Are you comfortable with the job description that was placed in the classified ad? Do you have questions?'

I quickly reviewed in my mind the job description from the job ad and answered his questions: 'No questions, Sir. The ad was quite descriptive of the duties and I am ready to start as soon as we discuss compensation.'

'Excellent', said Mr Luciferous, as he hands me a sheet of paper and I find the compensation package detailed in it. My jaw almost drops when I see the compensation sum, the super contribution, the holiday package. I think to myself, where do I sign!

'I find this compensation package to be acceptable, Mr Luciferous. When do I start?'

Mr Luciferous hands me another sheet of paper with the word 'Contract' as its title. I skimmed through it and found nothing distressful. I see that it just requires me to collect any debts because of Mr Luciferous, and that is it. Simple enough. Just locate the individuals that owes the debt and collect it. I sign on the spot and hand the contract back to Mr. Luciferous.

Mr. Luciferous gets up and turns to his left and goes to the bookcase and brings back an extensive file labelled with a single letter 'A' and hands it to me.

'Here you go, Albert. Start with this file and bring me back all these souls.'

TWO OF ME

Today I see myself between two worlds. Happy to be from both and often I dream, which is best for me. The country I have not seen in many years or the one I live in now. Two cultures. I do not want to choose. Two of me today and forever.

WHY DO I ENJOY WRITING

As I am pounding away on my computer keyboard, my wife asks me a simple question; "Why do you like to write?" A simple question: indeed, why do I like to write? It is not because I am a prolific and published writer; I am not, not yet. I want one day to publish an anthology of fiction, but that is not why I write.

There are several reasons writers write, some writers write to inform, like a journalist, some write to persuade or to give you, their opinion. Another writer may write to entertain, and most writers write to express themselves. This last reason is why I strive to become a writer. The stories I enjoy writing not only come out of the world I live in but also from another world, my imaginary world. A world in which I make these stories alive and sometimes in a world in which I want to live in and be a part of.

Whether it is a romance story, an adventure story, a science fiction story, or a murder mystery, these stories give me the chance to experience, in my way, a world which only a few individuals can experience.

My imagination allows me to be a spectator to a historical period in time or I may be the hero of a detective story or, even better yet, the romantic lead similar to "El Zorro" and who does not want to look like Antonio Banderas.

So, I let my imagination fly each day for at least an hour, sometimes a bit more and it transcends various levels of consciousness as I go from one scene to the next, one storyline to the next, ever-evolving, ever-changing but always, yes always, just my story and me.

ABOUT THE AUTHOR

José Nodar was born in La Habana, Cuba.

He grew up in a middle-class neighbourhood until the Cuban Revolution of 1959 threw a spanner into his happy life.

His parents heard a story that children under the age of eleven were to be sent to Russia for 'indoctrination.' This rumour was untrue, but they believed it to have been incited by the Catholic Archdiocese of Miami and the American Central Intelligence Agency under the title 'The Pedro Pan Project' or 'The Peter Pan Project.'

This led José to be one of the 14,000 children sent to the USA to disrupt Fidel Castro's regime, but it disrupted the lives of so many families instead.

In 1968 José's parents left Cuba under the 'Freedom Flights' (known in Spanish as Los Vuelos de La Libertad) and these flights transported about Cubans to Miami twice daily, five times per week from 1965 to 1973 and José and his parents reunited after all those years.

From 1968 to 1970 José and his parents lived and worked in San Juan Puerto Rico where they owned a restaurant, but this type of work proved unsatisfactory to José, and he headed back north to Atlanta Georgia where he had some friends and a possibility of a new job career.

This job career turned out to be in the banking arena and then into international consulting, which became the backbone of his professional life.

In 2008 the Great Financial Crisis (GFC) struck the financial world like Thor's hammer and José and his Australian wife (Miriam) moved to Australia and pursue their lives there.

In 2014, José and Miriam retired in Spring Farm, New South Wales (a Sydney suburb) and have enjoyed their retirement ever since while pursuing their hobbies and interests.

José Nodar ©   2021

CPSIA information can be obtained
at www.ICGtesting.com
Printed in the USA
BVHW042102231221
624755BV00013B/842